It all began with a WEDDING

USA TODAY BESTSELLING AUTHOR
H.M. SHANDER

Jennifer
your week is now
booked. :)
happy reading.
♡ hm shander
Sept 20

It All Began with a Wedding

Published by H.M. Shander

It All Began with a Wedding is a work of fiction. Names, characters, places and incidents either are the products of the author's imagination or are used factitiously. Any resemblances to actual persons, living or dead, events or locals, are entirely coincidental.

www.hmshander.com

Cover Design: Megan Parker @ EmCat Designs

Editing: Irina Mulholland @ IDIM Editorial

Proofreading: Victoria Brock @ The Word Tank

Shander, H.M., 1975—It All Began with a Wedding

May your time
between these pages
be as well spent as mine were
in writing them.

Table of Contents

Chapter One..1
Chapter Two..12
Chapter Three..22
Chapter Four..31
Chapter Five..46
Chapter Six..52
Chapter Seven..67
Chapter Eight..77
Chapter Nine..88
Chapter Ten..102
Chapter Eleven..111
Chapter Twelve..118
Chapter Thirteen..130
Chapter Fourteen..141
Chapter Fifteen..157
Chapter Sixteen..166
Chapter Seventeen..176
Chapter Eighteen..187
Chapter Nineteen..198
Chapter Twenty..202
Chapter Twenty-One..218
Chapter Twenty-Two..222
Chapter Twenty-Three..237
Epilogue..251
Dear Reader..258
Other Books..259
Acknowledgements..260
About The Author..262

Chapter One

Thursday, June 11th

I was minutes away from becoming the largest shareholder of a national chain of pharmacies. Minutes away from becoming richer than I'd ever dreamed and mere minutes away from my life changing forever. The worst part was, I wanted nothing to do with it.

"Miss Richardson, are you hearing what I'm saying?" The oldest-looking of the three men pulled off his wire-rimmed glasses, and with his other hand rubbed the bridge of his nose.

"Yes, sir."

"Would you care to repeat it back to me? This is an important matter and it's imperative that you fully understand." He glanced to the other two people: one on either side of him and all three staring across the table at me.

Carefully, and with the intent of coming across as much older than my twenty-seven years, I nodded. "If I'm to understand you correctly…" I glanced at the folders lined up neatly between us. "I am about to inherit my grandfather's shares of his pharmaceutical company Merryweather-Weston."

I didn't add that it was a company my grandfather Lloyd Merryweather started from the ground up in his late teens in the 1960s. When he married my grandmother Thelma Weston in 1965, he added her name to the business. Together, over the past fifty years, they grew their mom and pop corner store into a nationwide chain.

"That's correct." He reached for a file and opened it to a pinned page. "Go on."

I kept my sighs to myself. "As the - how did you put it - shareholder with the largest interest, I will hold 58% of the company's shares and stocks which are currently held in the family trust." My math was rusty and the numbers I'd written down at the start of the meeting were swimming around on the page. All I knew was that by having more than fifty percent, I was in charge, another thing I wasn't looking forward to. Running a business was so beyond my learning capabilities. Why hadn't Grandpa bothered to discuss this with me previously? Oh right. He wasn't supposed to have been killed.

An older gentleman sitting next to the lawyer, originally introduced as the accountant, who sat next to the lawyer, scribbled across a legal pad. "The correct percentage is 58.3." He didn't lift his eyes to connect with me.

That's what that number was. I circled it repeatedly to drive that home. Percentages with decimals were a big deal. As I looked around the boardroom, I was so out of my league, and every person in that room knew it. Growing up the way I had, I wasn't expected to follow in my single mother's footsteps and eventually run the business the way she had, not even when cancer took her away four years ago. She'd been on board though when I felt a calling into micro-biology and creating new drugs that would cure various illnesses. I wanted to be famous for finding a cure for cancer, not for running a well-known business.

Instead of toiling away in the lab, I was sitting with a lawyer, an accountant and whoever the third guy was, being forced to take ownership of the entire three thousand plus stores. Although the way they talked about the whole situation, it was already a done deal. They just needed my signature on a bunch of papers to make it official.

"Just so you're aware, Mr. Crowe, I know…"

"We are aware of your position, Miss Richardson.

With Mr. Merryweather's accident, this has been thrust upon you. The board of directors are willing to assist you however they can until you get on your feet, and the CFO is on board to bring you up to speed. This meeting is just to sign over the documents making you the President."

President, aka the largest shareholder. I cleared my throat. "And if I decide that I don't want to be the president of the company?" I belonged in the lab, wearing latex gloves and eye goggles, not in a boardroom, running a company. However, with my family all gone, it appeared I had little choice in the matter.

That blank expression the lawyer had worn for the last hour hadn't faded with my admission. "You are free and clear to sell off your shares as you see fit, after first offering them to the board of directors." He flipped through a stack of papers and retrieved a stapled package and set it in front of me.

There was so much I needed to learn. Why did Grandpa have to drive that day? If he'd only taken a ride from his service… I shook my head, feeling a tendril of hair sneak out of the clip and fall across the nape of my neck. So much for maintaining a professional look.

"Miss Richardson," said the only man in the room who really hadn't talked much over the past hour. So many different terms had come and gone that I couldn't remember what his position was. “If I may.” He pulled himself closer to the table and set down his pen. “This is a difficult time for you, and we’re all aware of how much information you are being bombarded with.”

At least someone had the decency to understand.

“In simple terms, you are now the largest shareholder of your grandfather’s company and you can be as involved as you wish. However, any changes you’d like to implement must pass through the board. The twelve members collectively hold the other 41.7% of the business. None of that will change, unless you wish to sell part or all of your shares. The only thing that has changed, at this point in time, is the name on the title. Merryweather-Weston will continue to operate in its excellent way with or without your input.”

My head was swirling with words and numbers and visions of a stuffy board room similar to the one I was in and a possible future where I’d be swimming with the sharks. Oh, how I needed to escape, even if just for a moment to catch my breath. There were no windows up here, no view to take in. Just dark grey walls giving the whole room an institutional feel. I twitched in my seat and buried my head in my hands. “I’m sorry, I just need time to process all of this. To be honest, I thought I was coming here to sign a few papers, not all this.” I wanted to add and *go my merry* way, but refrained and bit my lip instead.

The lawyer broke his staidness and cocked an eyebrow in my general direction.

The last guy pulled back another file with a tab that had my name on it and opened it. A stack of papers at least a half inch thick were neatly tucked inside. Were those all on me?

An unknown and unwelcome tightness squeezed around my chest.

A knock sounded on the door.

"Come in," the lawyer said.

A middle-aged man in a form-fitting suit walked in and dropped another file on the table. "Sorry to interrupt, but we found some information that changes the presidency of the company."

"Miss Richardson, this is Mr. Colby Pratt, one of the senior board members."

Mr. Pratt shook my hand with a giant Cheshire cat grin and turned his attention back to the lawyer. I'd never met the man previously, but his name was one tainted from overhearing Grandpa discuss business over the phone when he was at home. Mr. Pratt's name did not come with the affection of a grandfather talking with a grandson, instead it was met with disdain. Grandpa had wanted Mr. Pratt out of the business but he refused to'd sell.

"What did you find out?"

Mr. Pratt did not glance in my direction. "At the time of Ms. Nora Weston's passing, Mr. Merryweather updated his last will and testament and named Miss Richardson here as the sole inheritor."

Nora Weston was my mother, their former CEO who was as tough as nails.

"We have already established that."

"However, those shares are to be halved." Mr. Pratt puffed out his chest, straining the buttons on his already too-tight shirt. "As a lawyer, how did you not check out Miss Richardson's person?" He narrowed his eyes. "According to the Matrimonial Property Act, her shares would be equally split between her and husband, effectively diluting the ownership. With that division, including her shares owned previously, she would own 34.45% of the shares. As a shareholder with a personal share total of 35%, that would mean I'd become president." He pushed a stapled copy of papers in the lawyer's direction.

Matrimonial Act? Was that something worked out between Grandpa and Grandma? No wait a minute. He was referring to *my* shares. But I wasn't married.

I still hadn't even found the guy I'd want to share anything personal with, let alone spend the rest of my life with him. Married? The idea was crazy enough to make me laugh. But I held back.

Wait a minute!

Images flitted through my mind at light-speed. A cute guy. A convention back in the fall. Way too much booze.

The lawyer lifted the new document and flipped through them. “But she hasn’t announced an engagement, Mr. Pratt. I think you’re jumping the gun just a little. And if she were to get married, she can, *and should*, get a prenuptial.” He looked down his nose at me.

“She’s already married and there was no prenup.”

Everyone knew that marriages in Vegas were a farce. There needed to be a license and all that. One can’t simply go into any old chapel and get married without those things. Otherwise, it’s like performing a part of a play; it wasn’t real.

Mr. Pratt’s stupid grin got even bigger as he turned.

I balled my hands into tight little fists. Fight with the truth, Grandpa said, and you’ll always win. “It wasn’t legal.” I inhaled and tried to calm myself down. “Where’s the marriage license?”

Mr. Pratt flipped through his file and dropped a piece of paper on the table between the lawyer and me.

Clear as a bell on a beige wedding certificate from

the Cupid's Arrow Chapel was my name and the name of one Theodore Breslin.

That drunken night at a Vegas medical conference flashed through my mind again. There was no way anyone would have married us, we were too drunk to know how to spell our names, as evident in the spelling of mine. On the certificate, my name was spelled I-S-A-B-E-L-L-A, but in truth, the 's' was a 'z'.

The buttons on my blouse pulled against their holds as I inhaled rapidly. I couldn't be married. It can't be possible. I haven't even seen that guy since then.

"Miss Richardson?" The lawyer's voice seemed far away as if caught in a fog.

My hand wiped the building sweat off my forehead, taking all my composure with it. "Yeah?" Grandpa would have smacked my backside for answering an elder like that.

"I guess that solves your dilemma."

"What's that?"

"You said you didn't want to be president, and now you don't have to worry about that. You'll remain on board as a minor shareholder, but not the president."

It sounded as if I should've been happy about the news of a marriage to a guy I didn't recall saying 'I do' to, but the smug look on Mr. Pratt's face wiped away the smidgen of joy I may have held for the briefest of heartbeats. Not only did he resemble a weasel, he acted like it too. A burst of adrenaline coursed through me. Yeah, maybe I didn't want to run the company, but I'll be damned if I was going to turn it over to him. Grandpa really disliked him.

I faced the lawyer. "If I get a divorce, how does that work?"

"By law, if there was no prenup, he'd still be entitled to half."

Right, that whole Matrimonial Act and all. That wouldn't solve issue number one. I needed to think. A drunken marriage. I was sure there were more of those than not. How many ended up not being legit? Probably low. I tapped my head. Wasn't there a celebrity who married in Vegas and got it annulled? "What about an annulment? Then that would dissolve the marriage and all assets remained would be mine, correct?"

Mr. Pratt's face fell. Good.

The lawyer shuffled a few papers around and scribbled on his legal pad. "Provided you and…" He reached for the marriage certificate. "Mr. Breslin meet certain criteria."

"Like? Is being drunk enough to not remember reason enough?"

"It stacks the deck in your odds." He finally made eye contact with me but after first glancing up at Mr. Pratt.

The prick had the audacity to laugh. "She'll never get in front of a judge in time."

"Why's that?"

"Because Miss Richardson…" He opened his file and flipped to a page tagged with a yellow tab, "if you'd read section 198.14 – and I'll summarize this for you – it basically states that even though the estate is frozen, there is a 60 day grace period to find an interim president. With your assets now in half, I legally become the president, and there are only fifteen days left to contest." I could almost imagine Grandpa saying he'd smack that look off the smug bastard's face. The thought made me smile.

"Well, let's get that process started, so I can get before a judge. I'll need a minute with you, in private, please," I addressed the lawyer.

"Absolutely."

An hour later, I left the high-rise building in the heart of our downtown a different person. Not only was I married, but I had a less than two weeks to find my husband, get an annulment before the judge Mr. Crowe had graciously set up for me, and retain major shares in the business I barely understood in order to keep Mr. Pratt's greasy hands off it. Over the morning, I'd aged ten years.

Chapter Two

Friday, June 12th

Even with scouring social media, it took me a bit of time to locate the whereabouts of one Theodore Breslin. Knowing he was in the medical field did help narrow him down, and after locating the clinic where he worked, I managed to squeeze in an end of the day appointment, thanks to the accommodating receptionist. I hated how I used my sweetest voice to secure the meeting and stretched the truth about being in the pharmaceutical department with an important new treatment I'd like him to see. It took a moment to convince her it was just Dr. Breslin, and not the entire staff at the clinic I wanted to see.

Five minutes before my booked time, I walked into the bright and airy entrance devoid of that typical antiseptic clean smell of most clinics. The space had a more natural scent which I assumed belonged to the abundance of potted greenery.

All business, I came dressed in the same clothing I wore to the lawyers – a black pencil skirt and pantyhose, and a white blouse with a blazer over top. Somehow, I managed to get my hair into a more appropriate chignon as opposed to the ponytail I was known to sport. My cheeks even had a smidgen of blush on them, enough to make my mom proud, and when I left my apartment, I was the spitting image of her.

Trying to keep the clicking of my heels to a minimum, I trekked across the tile floor over to the sweet receptionist. “I have a four-thirty appointment with Dr. Breslin.” My sweaty palm wrapped tighter around the handle of the carrying case loaded with files and paperwork.

“He’s just finishing up with a patient, but Louise will take you back in a few minutes.”

“Perfect.” I paced over to the window, and scanned the new buildings growing around, my focus darting to the downtown on the horizon. It wasn’t enough to keep my nervous energy at bay, so I sat in one of the empty chairs and crossed my legs, the free leg bouncing in the air.

“Leonard?” The nurse called out.

The only other patient in the room, an elderly man, grunted and shifted the tubing connecting him to the oxygen tank he carried. He pushed himself to a stand, one of the tubes catching on the corner of his chair.

"Just wait," I told him, and hunched down to unhook it. "Let me help you." I lifted the various plastic tubes as he shuffled over to the nurse and passed them over to her.

The older man with a head full of grey hair turned to me and patted my arm. Words came out of his mouth, but I didn't understand them. However, I did understand the smile in his eyes.

He took off and a minute later the nurse returned. "Izabella?"

Shoulders back, I walked past the reception desk and into an exam room. If only my insides matched the false confidence of my outsides. Inside, I was a heart-pounding, fast breathing, stomach-knotted mess. My blood pressure had to be off the charts as well.

"And what are you here to see Dr. Breslin about?" She held a sticky pad in her left hand and a pen poised to write down whatever ailments I could be suffering with.

"I have some paperwork to go over with him." I tapped my carrying case for good measure. "Would we be able to sit in an office or a boardroom? An exam room isn't necessary."

She tucked her writing supplies into her scrub top. "Sure." Her words hung in the air with hesitation. "I can take you to his office."

"Thank you." I tried to use my sweetest voice but considering I looked like a cheap knockoff of Miranda Priestly, I doubted she heard the sincerity in my voice.

His office was in the back corner of the clinic, as if it were almost an afterthought. The desk took up half the space and was littered with files upon files. There was barely enough room for a couple of chairs in front, and that's where the nurse pointed.

I took a seat and put the carrying case across my lap. She left the door open as she exited.

Personal effects around the closet-sized room were in short supply and the piles of clutter were not helping my anxiety. The bookcase behind me had stacks of books and medical journals and two 3D models: one of a set of lungs and one of the female reproductive system. The walls were covered in diplomas from various graduating schools. This clinic had four doctors working in it, all of whom graduated before I was born. I took a closer look at Dr. Breslin's diploma, since he would obviously be the young buck around here. He earned his M.D. last spring which, in theory, would put him at around the same age as me, assuming he didn't take a gap year between high school and university. For some reason that put my mind at ease, although my memories didn't peg him as an older man.

A knock sounded against the open door, and I spun around to see if it was intended for me. A tall and handsome man, with light brown hair and brown eyes that pierced my soul, greeted me as he walked into the space. Suddenly a flood of fun memories washed over me.

"Dr. Breslin?" My voiced cracked and in the next heartbeat, I cleared my throat. I only asked to be sure it was actually him, although my heart knew it was. How could I have forgotten that gorgeous face?

"Yes." He stood at the door in track pants and a scrub shirt, a stethoscope hanging around his neck. Next to him, I was so overdressed it was ridiculous. What I'd give to be in comfy pants and my scrubs.

"Hi, Izabella Richardson." I extended my hand. A warm, soft grip did not disappoint me.

"What can I help you with today?" His voice was all business. Damn.

My heart fell. Clearly, he did not remember me the way my body remembered him. My heart pounded so fiercely, I was surprised I could hear him talk. "We met back in Las Vegas at the Pharmaceutical convention."

If he recalled anything, his face didn't show it. Part of the medical training, I was sure. Don't show emotions. Something I was learning very hard to do.

He gave me a slow nod. "Izabella…" My name

never sounded so melodic.

"Yes, if it's okay with you, I have some important things to discuss with you. In private. Do you have fifteen minutes?" I purposely made sure to book the last appointment of the day so as to not take away time from patients who truly needed him, but sometimes emergencies happened and that never worked out.

"For you, of course." His gaze fell to the carrying case. "Have a seat." He closed the door after pushing the door stop out of the way.

I sat in one of the vinyl-covered seats and crossed my legs. "I suppose you don't remember me?"

The eyes gave nothing away and it was killing me. There was no flicker of recognition. "You look familiar, and your name rings a bell, but if you forgive my ignorance, Miss Richardson was it? I see people all the time."

"Right, of course you do." I unzipped the carrying case, tucking my emotions deep into my gut. Not going to lie, it stung just a little bit that he didn't know who I was. "Well, you not remembering me does make the whole thing easier." I pulled out the pages I'd picked up from Mr. Crowe's secretary and placed it in the clear space between us.

"What's this?" Dr. Breslin picked up the package

and while maintaining his impassive expression, his eyes scanned the document. "For real?"

"We have a court date for June 23rd, to make our petition before the judge. Being that you don't remember me, and I had no idea a marriage preformed while severely intoxicated was legally binding, my lawyer is confident we'll get the annulment."

"I'm married?" The words were barely a whisper.

"For what it's worth, Dr. Breslin, I was a little shocked as well."

Finally, a ghost of emotion floated behind his eyes, and like a zap of electricity, it was gone.

"I'm making this as easy for you as possible. My lawyer has drawn up the papers, and you'll need to sign where all the tags are and add your own declaration. I can give you the weekend to look over the paperwork and can swing by on Monday to pick it up." I'd flipped through his copy and most of the pertinent info was blank; full name, contact info, that kind of thing. I really had nothing on the guy. Provided he did his part, the annulment process should be a walk in the park.

"How did you find out?" He looked me square in the eyes.

How I found out was none of his business, even if this stranger was technically my husband. Finding a way to tread this was going to be difficult. I re-crossed my legs and pulled back. “All you need to know is that it was brought to my attention yesterday.”

There was a slight cock of his head to the right as he took in my blunt statement. “So, you had no idea? You didn’t remember?”

I pushed my shoulders down and brushed my bangs away from my eyes. “Until the marriage certificate was produced, no, I’d completely forgotten about that evening.” However, the memories were rolling in fast and steady like waves on a beach.

“What do you recall?”

My head tipped a little and I looked him in the eyes, my voice sagging at the hazy images. “Honestly, not a lot. The finer details escape me. I know we’d met a couple days earlier at a lecture put on by Merryweather-Weston featuring the prominent researcher Dr. Lisa Lowe.” She’d been so passionate about the discoveries made within the DNA of damaged cells it was inspiring and fueled my own research, sending me down a different path than the one I’d been on.

“She was quite lively.”

“And afterwards, we went out with a group of researchers and cruised the strip, drinking to excess. Things get a little fuzzy after the pool. There was lots of laughing and drinks served in baseball bats. The wedding ceremony details are blurry at best. All I can remember is your face, some truly horrible music playing in the chapel and how bad it smelled."

"Probably vomit."

How could I have been so naïve? Squeezing my hands together, I composed myself. "I should have left and dragged you out with me. I was so drunk they even spelled my name wrong, and had I been in a better state of mind, I know I would have corrected them. Putting an 's' instead of a 'z' has always been a sore spot." My eyes drifted to the package I'd given him. "There's a copy of the marriage certificate on the last page."

He flipped to it and gave it a read, the only sound being a slight wheeze coming from him with his deep sigh.

My phone vibrated in the pocket of my blazer, a signal that my fifteen minutes was up. "Well, Dr. Breslin, it's time for me to go. My number, as well as that of my lawyer, is included on your copy. However, if you have any questions, he would be your best bet." I rose and smoothed out the crease that had formed across the front of my skirt. "Does Monday afternoon work for me to pick it up?" I slipped around the chair and took two steps to the closed door.

He stared at me. "This is real?" The package waved

in his hands.

“I’m sorry to tell you it is.”

“I see.”

“I’ll be back on Monday. Court date is the 23rd. Judge will see us both at 10:20. Please don’t be late.”

My grandpa’s company depends on you being there and signing the papers.

Chapter Three

Saturday, June 13th

With a cereal bowl full of breakfast, I lounged over to the coffee table and flipped on my PVRed show *Survivor.* Three episodes behind, and having avoided all spoilers on social media, I had big plans on getting caught up this morning. There was nothing pressing for once on my schedule; the lab could wait for a bit. Leaning against the back of the couch, I propped my bare feet upon the coffee table and held the bowl close to my face.

A dribble of milk trickled down my chin when a soft knock sounded on the door. It was likely Alberta, the older neighbour down the hall who liked to bake on the weekend and usually ran out of something mid-pie or cookie. It was so habitual, I made sure to stock extra baking items for her weekly visits, and she rewarded me with a container of whatever she'd created. Win-win for us both.

I gave my chin a wipe with my sleeve. "Just a second." I set my bowl beside a steaming latte, hoping my Froot Loops wouldn't be soggy upon my return and pressed the pause button.

I tugged down my oversized hoodie and straightened out my capris, reaching for the door. "Hey," I said and just about added *Mrs. Grabbenstein*. Instead, the perfect body of a hot doctor stood in front of me.

Dressed in a nice shirt and wrinkle-free shorts, he smiled. "Good morning."

I glanced down the hall, wondering if this was a joke, and turned back to half-smile at him. "How did you?"

"I followed someone in."

Perhaps I needed to post a sign in the lobby that ALL visitors needed to be buzzed up and not slipped in. It was a huge breach of security. Instead of laying into him, I simply nodded and narrowed my eyes. "How did you know where I lived?"

He waved the manila-coloured envelope in his hands. "Your address is on the annulment papers."

"Right." I was sure that pretty boy doctor was now thinking he didn't marry the sharpest tack in the box and was probably uber-thankful for the upcoming annulment. "Come on in?" I asked and stepped aside. There was no way I was going to be less than polite now. "Can I get you something to drink? I can whip you up a latte or something."

"Sure, a latte would be nice." He stood at the edge of my galley kitchen while I prepped the machine and made him the best damn milky coffee he'd ever have. I got so involved in making sure it was near perfect that if he spoke, I didn't hear anything.

He laughed as I handed the glass mug to him.

"What's so funny?"

"I've seen doctors in surgery who are less laser-focused than you were making me a cup of coffee."

"Ugh, I truly hope not, and I'd like their names should ever I fall under needing their services." I pushed by him gently and made my way over to my seat. My cereal had long passed the edible level and it was time to dispose of it. "Excuse me." I dumped it into the sink and returned to my spot on the couch. "So, Dr. Breslin, what's on your mind? Was something not clear in the document?" My eyes fell to the manila envelope.

"Yes and no." He took a quick sip; a little mustache of foam covered his upper lip.

I couldn't remove my gaze from it, and there was no logical reason why I should be staring so much, but something about the way it sat there, well, it was slightly endearing. He cleared his throat and my eyes refocused on his. "You were saying?"

"Yes, everything seems crystal clear as far as the dates and reasons for asking for the annulment." The last word lingered in the air.

"Excellent." I nearly clapped my hands in joy.

"I'm just not sure about it."

My eyebrow jumped sky high. "About the justice of the peace that allowed two overly drunk people to enter into a binding contract of matrimony?"

"Well, there's that." His gaze fell to the envelope and his shoulders rolled inward.

I lifted my cooled-down latte and had a sip while waiting for the good doctor to explain what he wasn't clear about.

Dr. Breslin also claimed a taste of his milky espresso and set it down, moving it around in small circles.

"Dr. Breslin, is there something I can explain to help make this easier?"

"Please, call me Theo."

Irises as brown as melted chocolate stared at me, rendering me speechless. Their power was intoxicating, and it was amazing I could make myself nod.

As if he didn't understand the pull he suddenly had over me, he spoke. "Last night, I read over the document multiple times, and I stared at the copy of the wedding certificate, and memories started flooding back."

That I understood. This whole wedding thing had been in the forefront of all my thoughts lately. It had been a giant mistake to:

a) get that drunk, especially with a guy I barely knew and

b) marry someone when I should've known better.

I was just super thankful that we'd never consummated the ceremony (one of the first reasons for the annulment). At least my brain had chosen a marriage partner well. He was clearly smart, and a fine specimen of a man. It's too bad I didn't get to know him as a person, although I supposed if he was a decent man, that could've made it harder to reject the marriage. But since I didn't know…

"And the thing is, and this is probably going to sound weird."

Not likely. When old friends discover you working in pharmaceuticals – even though you don't dispense the actual drugs – it's amazing the ailments they are willing to share with you in the hopes you will be able to get them, or at the very least tell them, which ones would be most effective. However, I didn't want to interject into his conversation, so I let him carry on.

"I've never been married before, and I always

thought I would bring a girl home to the family first and if they loved her as much as I did, that I'd get their blessing to approach her father and ask for his daughter's hand. I'm that kinda guy."

I thrust my hand up, not liking the direction he was headed, even if the words were the sweetest I'd heard. I'd pretty much thought that level of charm went the way of the Cold War. Honest to God, there were still guys like that out there? "There's probably a reason we skipped the step of meeting my father and all that jazz." I laughed out loud since it was funny to me. "I don't know who my father even is."

He cocked his head off to the side and looked at me as though I'd just spoken a string of Arabic.

"It's not important." I shook my head. All my mom ever said was that it had been the best mistake of her life, and she left it at that. She was going to double love me for the both of them. "Sorry. Continue."

He took another small sip and held tightly onto his mug. "My point being, all my life, that was my dream of the perfect lead up to the engagement, and we missed a few steps."

I chuckled and took a long drink from my mug. "Did we ever." Like the whole dating and trying each other on for size. I didn't have a ring, hadn't gone dress shopping with my girls, hadn't even checked him out in the sack.

He wasn't laughing, and suddenly, my heart rate kicked up a notch. His hand fell onto the envelope. "I know. Sorry. I assume there will be a giant protest if I refuse the annulment."

You got that right. As much as I wanted to let the words fly out, I reigned them in and twisted my hands in my lap.

"So… I'm willing to reach a compromise." He hung his head. "I'll give in to the annulment, but I'd like you to meet my family first."

"Are you serious?" Even though I didn't know him per se, his stern look told me he was dead serious. "What would that even accomplish? Wouldn't it be easier if we continued on the path we're on – that of two strangers who made a mistake? Cut the ties that bind us and go our merry way?" That was the best-case scenario in my head. No muss, no fuss, just done. Then I could direct my energies toward figuring out the whole Mr. Pratt board member situation and finding a solution to that problem. First step though was making sure I remained in control.

"I think it would be great for my parents to meet you, at least once. We wouldn't have to say a word about the impromptu wedding, just that you are Izabella." He said it as if my name was a regular in conversation.

"And after the court date?" I just couldn't see how this was going to work. There were too many holes in his plan.

"We broke up."

"And your parents, they won't see right through that?"

He shook his head. "Nope."

"And what do I get out of this meeting?"

He lowered his head and practically looked at me through his eyebrows. "Are you kidding me?" His finger tapped the envelope on the table.

Right, the annulment. Could I do it? Could I meet the parents of the man I wanted an annulment from? Meeting his parents wouldn't accomplish anything in the grand scheme of things, it was just a lunch or dinner. Simple enough, right? However… "I still don't understand though, why meet your parents? Why get anyone outside of us involved?"

"Because I'm a family guy."

I crinkled my nose at him. It still wasn't much of an answer.

"I've been an outcast all my life. Always different than my siblings and cousins. Just this once, I want to bring a lady home to meet them so they can see I'm maybe not so different."

Not so different. Words I could stand behind. “Fine.” Breath raced over my lips. “When?”

A broad smile spread across his face. “Do you have plans next Saturday night?”

Chapter Four

It was utter lunacy agreeing to meet his family, and I could hear the tsking coming from my best friend Camille when I told her, but for the sake of Grandpa's company, I was in. "Sure, next Saturday works."

"Great. It's my cousin's wedding."

Well, flip me over. I expected to meet his parents, and maybe a sibling. Guess he took family to be all-encompassing, and suddenly I was about to meet everyone. The whole shebang. "A wedding? Couldn't we start with something smaller, like a dinner or something?"

"Looking at the court date and my schedule and based on what I assume is a busy schedule for you, Saturday is about the only availability."

I tugged at my collar and billowed my hoodie. "Is it a big wedding?"

"Five hundred people, give or take?"

I gave him a slow nod. “Great.” The fakest smile ever formed pushed my ample cheeks higher. Hopefully, I’d get lost in the sea of people and no one would remember me. Who is his cousin? The Duke or Duchess of Edmonton? Five hundred guests were a lot of people. I don’t think I knew that many people, including all my work connections and the shop owners working under Grandpa’s banner – something I’d need to work on in the coming months.

“It’ll be fine. I appreciate you doing this for me.”

“Likewise.” For the sake of the business.

“In the meantime, do you think we can hang out and get to know one another? It would lend itself to our relationship being more authentic.” He took a long sip of his latte and held my gaze firmly.

I tore my focus away; the pleading look was too much to take. I wasn’t sure about us trying to be more real. I wanted the relationship over, not starting out from scratch. The quicker we cut the ties, the better. When we stood before the judge, it needed to be crystal clear that we barely knew each other.

His gaze travelled over my face, and I hoped I hid my emotions well enough that he couldn’t see the wavering I was committing.

I lifted my mug to my lips and tipped back the rest,

staring absently into the bottom where the milky fluid ran in rivulets across the empty bottom.

"Can I be honest with you?" The words flew out of my mouth before I had a chance to stop them.

He sat up straighter, as if he was expecting bad news. Which was partially true, I wasn't about to sugar coat anything. He cleared his throat. "Oh god, you have a boyfriend, don't you? Why didn't I think that through? How silly of me. I'm sorry."

I laughed as he dropped his gaze to the floor and rolled his shoulders inward. "Oh god, no. There's no boyfriend." My life was too full to even entertain the idea of trying to keep a man happy. It was hard enough trying to squeeze in dinner dates with best friends who knew about my busy life and allowed the lack of communication to grow.

Relief covered him and he relaxed a teeny bit.

But he certainly could be in a relationship, and a tiny ember of jealousy flared at the thought. "What about you?"

"No," he said matter-of-factly. "I don't have a girlfriend."

Not sure why that made my heart skip a beat. Not that it mattered. "Okay."

"I just want to be friends. Considering we are

technically a married couple, the least we could do is get to know each other better."

"Unfortunately, that's where you're wrong. When we stand before the judge declaring how we never consummated our marriage, that we were strangers and exceptionally drunk at the time of signing the marriage certificate, we need to be seen keeping our distance."

"I don't think us knowing a little of the other is going to affect the outcome of the divor… annulment."

I shrugged. "I can't chance that. There needs to be no shadow of a doubt that the annulment is a given, and the whole thing was a gigantic mistake."

"Was it a mistake?" An underlying current of hurt was there.

"Yes, it was." I set my cup down with a little more force than intended, and a surprised Theo pulled back. "Look, I have a mean streak and I'm a high maintenance woman. There's a list a mile long of why I don't have a boyfriend, and I add to it daily."

He finished off his latte and rose, grabbing the envelope. On his way to the door, he put his mug into the sink. "I've never been one to back down from a challenge. Besides, as much as I believe that you don't have a boyfriend *at the moment,* I think you're lying about the mean streak and maintenance part. I'll find a way to prove that we can be friends, Izabella."

I joined him and leaned against the wall. "At the risk of being rude, Theo, I have enough friends."

"Then, what it is you'd like?" There was such sincerity in his face it was hard to turn my head away.

What I'd like is to maintain control of the family business, find a way to reduce Mr. Pratt's stake in the company and figure out how the hell to run that and still do what I love doing. "I honestly can't answer that."

He put his hand on the doorknob. "Can't answer, or won't?"

"Both."

"Too bad." If there was one thing I didn't like, it was a cocky, self-assured man.

"Text me the details for the wedding, and we can work out travel arrangements."

"I'm sure I'll talk to you before that." He winked, the overhead light sparkling on the shine of his eyes.

"I'm sure you will." But I had no idea what that meant. Instead, after he stepped through the threshold, I closed the door and shook my head. What a dreamer.

# # #

All morning long, I just couldn't get the image of

the hot doctor out of my head and the sweet idea that we could be friends without it messing up the annulment. No matter what I did, he was there in every thought. As if I didn't have enough on my mind already.

Needing the distraction that getting into my research would bring me, I headed to the lab. At least there was a cooler full of cells I could dissect to try to unlock the cure I knew was hidden amongst the DNA. That seemed easier than trying to figure out the current state of my life.

Three hours later, my phone went off. A reminder set to have a bottle of water and a high-protein snack. I'd been known to go hours without eating or drinking, and discovered the hard way how it deeply affected my work and concentration. A quick alarm, a fast bite, and I was good to go again.

My phone buzzed again. Right in the middle of an application. A quick glance to the wall clock. The alarm wasn't supposed to go off yet. Sighing and knowing the work I felt I was making strides on was down the shitter now that I'd been interrupted, I grabbed the plastic bag the phone was stored in and lifted it up to see the display. The number was unrecognizable and in anger for being pulled out of my zone, I threw the bagged phone across the desk.

Blinking a few times to prime my eyes, I once again zoomed in on the single cell on the slide and retrieved my aspirating needle. That embedded DNA was all mine. The needle was just making contact when my phone buzzed again.

"Oh, for crying out loud." I launched myself at the damn device. The same number again. I tapped the answer button. "Yes?" I probably should've answered nicer, but geezus, what a time to interrupt.

"Izabella?" The voice was oddly familiar, but through the baggie it wasn't going to be crystal clear. It couldn't be the lawyer's office or a member of the board, although I wouldn't have put it past Mr. Pratt to call me on a Saturday at supper time.

"This is she." My voice softened. Work was halted anyways. I set the needle down.

"Hey, didn't recognize you there for a minute. It's Theo."

I tipped my head back and stared up at the ceiling. *Seriously?* "Hey, what's up?"

"Not much, you?"

"I'm in the middle of pulling DNA from a chromosome."

"No way. That's really cool."

And he would be the first person, aside from my

colleagues, to think that. My friends figured I was trying to play God by digging deep into the structure, which was the furthest thing from the truth. I didn't want people to suffer the way my mom did.

"Are you finishing up soon?"

"To be honest, I hadn't planned on it. I was thinking it would be me and an electron microscope for the night." Most of my Saturday nights were spent in the lab. It was my time and typically, I was undistracted. And will be again once I put my phone on silence.

"Well, I was thinking I could take you out for dinner. Nothing fancy. Not even something that a friend would go to, just a quick bite to eat. Like a burger or something."

The man was relentless, but my stomach betrayed me with a hardy growl. However, I blamed the thought of a juicy burger with all the fixings and a drippy, greasy mess. It actually sounded appealing.

"Hmmm…" There was so much to do, and it felt like I was seeing the light at the end of the tunnel. If I quit now, I'd have to restart the retraction process from scratch tomorrow. It took so long just to get to this point.

"Is that delay a yes?"

"It's a no," I said, surprisingly upset with myself. "I'm right in the depths of a project."

“That’s too bad.”

Suddenly, I was upset for the sadness in his voice, since I was responsible for it. “I’d apologize, but this research is very important to me.”

“Can I ask what you are working on?”

“I’m trying to find a cure for cancer.” If he laughed at me, it was soundless. Everyone normally did. It was the dream, right? Even that Amazon owner was trying to develop a cure. Wish I had his financial stability, though. The things I could do with access to that kind of money.

“That’s very noble of you.”

“Not general cancer, but more specifically pancreatic cancer.”

“Someone close to you?”

I allowed the line to stay silent. Already I’d said too much and given away too much about me personally.

“For what it’s worth, I’m sorry.” There was a genuine concern to his voice.

The final memories of my mom, withering away to nothingness in a hospital bed, flew to life like a movie that had been turned on. She’d wasted away to skin and bones in such a short time, it was shocking. There wasn’t an ounce of fat on her body to sustain her, and the damn cancer at her core quickly manifested and infected the organs around it, working in a sick partnership to end her beautiful life. There will never be another like her; she was indeed a one of a kind. Her absence had left a giant hole in my heart, the aching loneliness a daily reminder of what was missing in my life.

Maybe Theo was as lonely as I was. After all, of all the people he could be hanging with on a Saturday night, he was asking me. I shuddered to think there were two of us lonely souls; one was plenty. “If you’d like to watch me extract the DNA, come by the lab at the university.”

“Done.”

I pin dropped him the location as it was tucked away in the back part of the campus and went back to studying my first specimen under the scope.

The structure of the DNA was so amazing and intricate in the way the two pairs of bases connected and how each connection was responsible for making every human different from another. The chromosome I was working on extracting the DNA from, contained the genes I personally wanted to study. Not that it hadn’t been done before and mapped out. But these cells and chromosomes belonged to my mother and I was damned determined to see where the cancer had started out its mutation – the first piece of the puzzle had to be hidden in there. Maybe then we’d be able to develop a way to stop it before it even thought about changing.

A while later, the door at the back of the lab rang, and I walked through the double doors, out to the main door. Peeking through the spy hole, I spotted Theo and opened up for him.

"Hey."

He lifted up a bag that I'd smelled before I saw it. "I brought dinner."

"Come in." Once he was inside, the door sealed shut. "We can eat in the staff room. The room I'm working in is a clean room. No food allowed."

"Can't wait to see it."

I led him through another door into the staff room. The room itself was plain in nature; three long rows of tables filled the center, a bank of lockers on one wall, another wall had a fridge, small counter and a sink. Alongside the wall with the door was the Wall of Achievement with a strand of DNA between multiple awards given to the researchers and students.

Thankfully he ignored that as he stepped to the first table and sat. One by one, he pulled out a variety of items and set them down. "In the interest of not getting to know you better," he started off saying with a wink, "and not knowing what you liked, I grabbed a few different things."

There were two burgers, a mixed greens container, a box of fries and a side of gravy. My colleague, a health nut of a vegan, would've had a field day seeing and smelling all the grease.

"I'm surprised a doctor of all people would eat this." I pointed to the spread of artery-clogging food.

"It's not an everyday thing, that's for sure. But a little indulgence never hurt either. In fact, one would even say it's good for one's mental health to not deny it."

I reached for a napkin and dropped a handful of fries onto it. "Thanks for bringing me something to eat."

"My pleasure."

"You really had no place else to be?" Because it was highly doubtful that a guy as good looking as Theo had no one else to hang with aside from a lonely lab tech.

He shook his head. "Sad, right?"

"More like unbelievable."

He shrugged and crossed his fingers over his heart. "Total truth."

I started to feel some sort of weird connection to this husband of mine and I laughed internally at the thought. I knew more about my colleague's food choices, than I did about the man – my husband – sitting across from me. But still, there were some obvious similarities between us. Slowly, I unwrapped one of the burgers and took a nice-sized bite. It was just as juicy as I'd imagined.

"So, you like all the fixings on a burger, eh?" He

was just starting to unwrap his. "You didn't even look to see what was in there."

On that, I pulled the bun away from the burger. Nothing unusual. Lettuce, tomatoes, cheese, banana peppers. Well, that'll affect me later, but they always added a little something to whatever I was eating. "Looks good. Thank you. My usual work lunches consisted of bagel sandwiches and a baggie each of cut up fruit and veggies."

"They're from Barn's." He took a bite and swallowed. "In case you ever want to go there."

I nodded and took another bite, grease dribbling down my chin. I reached for a napkin and dabbed up the mess. "So, Theo, what would a guy like you normally do for fun, when you're not bringing burgers to a nerd?"

"Well, when I'm not a *Skip the Dishes* driver," he gave me the sweetest smile, "I like relaxing in my apartment, hanging out with my cat, who I've called Kitty."

"Kitty? Really?"

A little chunk of seasoning was visible between his teeth when he smiled.

"Yep. She's never told me her name, but she always comes when I say 'here, Kitty, Kitty'." He laughed.

"That's actually pretty awesome." I'd never had a

pet growing up. Mom always said they were a massive undertaking and there wasn't a whole lot of time for either one of us to devote to raising a pet.

"Maybe someday you'll get to meet her. Although, I need to ask, are you a dog person?"

"Not at all."

"Perfect. It's like she can sense that. Dog people really ruffle her fur."

"I'll keep that in mind." The likelihood of me ever going over to Theo's house was as remote as me finding the cure for pancreatic cancer while sitting in the staff room of the lab. I cast my gaze away from him and focused on the refrigerator tucked near the far wall; there was a note written in dry erase marker on the face of the fridge reminding people to remove their lunch bags at the end of the day.

With my tummy full, I gathered up our garbage and tossed it in the receptacle. After wiping the table down with a disinfectant wipe, I pointed to the lab. "Want to see what I'm working on?"

"I can do that?" His eyes lit up like a kid on Christmas morning.

"Sure, you can." I pounded a set of lockers for good measure. "You can put your belongings inside, not that anyone else is here…" I glanced around the empty room.

"And grab a lab coat and some gloves over there." The edge of a pair of blue nitrile gloves stuck out of the box and I grabbed those, pulling them on.

Theo donned a jacket that was a tad too small, but the gloves fit him perfectly.

"The room is a level ISO8. No need for decontamination or anything."

He nodded. "Show me the way."

Chapter Five

Since I'd eaten, and eaten well, I actually went longer than my normal three hours without a break, but Theo was such an amazing student, and hungry for all the information, that time flew by. I took him on a microscopic tour of the cell's structure and showed him the molecular differences between a regular cell and one infected by cancer, as well as how a virus attached to a healthy cell.

We exited the clean room back into the staff room, tossed our gloves, and rehung our lab coats. "Well, that was just plain cool."

"You don't see that with your patients, do you?"

"I've seen them with the side effects of many viruses, but I've never seen the viruses on that level." He was rocking on his feet, his face all lit up.

Theo was like how I thought I was back in the early days of university, where everything was brand new, and seeing it just added a whole other level of excitement.

He walked over to the bank of lockers and grabbed his belongings, before walking around the room. “Wait a sec.” He paused at the Wall of Accomplishments.

I’d hoped he wouldn’t be curious enough to look over the wall.

“Is that you?” He ran his finger over one of the frames. “And you’re there too.” Briefly he tore his gaze away and turned his attention to me. “How many?”

“There are five.” Five awards. Two were given to my team and me, nothing to catch the eye of the Nobel Prize Award committee though, as they were given from the head of the department. The three others around it? Those were given to me personally. I was the youngest recipient of the University’s Georges deMilo award for advances in pharmacological research, and that’s where I hoped my Nobel Prize would spring from.

“Incredible.” The words fell off his lips as he scanned the awards.

“Actually,” I wrapped my jacket around my shoulders and tucked my chin to my chest. “The others up there are much more incredible than me. Gino there,” I pointed towards the name in the centre, “he’s going to be the next Sir Alexander Fleming and discover the next penicillin-like drug.” And he was so close, too. He worked in a different part of the lab from me, but many times I'd heard Grandpa mention Gino's name and how he needed to keep an eye on him. Grandpa wanted that drug first, if Gino managed to discover it. "It's getting late. Shall we?"

"Thanks again for showing me the things you work on. You have an amazing job. On the front line of defence, like a soldier."

Theo stood beside me as I locked the facility behind us. There was a hint of dusk in the summer air; a sweet scent that comes with the setting sun as the heat of the day cools. The sun hadn't disappeared yet, but hung low enough so it wasn't visible above the trees. It gave off enough light however that not all the streetlights had started to turn on.

I gave a quick look over to Theo. "What about you? You're on the front line too. You're the one people come to when they're ill, the one people depend on."

"Are you kidding?"

"You heal people; how amazing is that?" I was trying to find a way to accomplish that on a molecular level.

"Well, I won't lie. It is pretty cool when a kid comes in with an ear infection, and I can make them feel better by prescribing the antibiotics that were created *in a lab.*"

"Not by me. At least not yet, although you'd have to be in oncology to use anything that I'm hoping to create but I'm working on it. Watson and Crick are my heroes, as are Banting and Best." The first two discovered DNA and the latter two discovered insulin. "And well, if we're talking about heroes, my grandparents and my mom are mine too." Wow. I stopped talking and blinked a few times. What was it about Theo that caused me to share more information with him than I had done with my girls? Pretty sure, Camille and Tess didn't know who my heroes are.

He led us away from the back of the building, out into a more open area of campus. "That's sweet. You must've been really close to your mom."

I looked deep into his eyes, seeing comfort in them. "Yes, we were very close." My heart ached. It just wasn't fair. But I shook the feeling away. Regardless of the undivided attention he was giving me to share, this wasn't the time nor the place. "What about you? Any heroes to speak of?"

"Not really."

"No destiny that called you into medicine?" I thought most people went into that field because it was a family field; they came from a long lineage of doctors and nurses.

Something I said rattled him just a touch. He straightened himself out and looked off far into the distance. “I come from a long line of lawyers. My grandfather was a lawyer, my father’s a lawyer and even my siblings are lawyers. I’m the black sheep of the family. Going into medicine ruffled a few feathers.”

“There’s nothing wrong with medicine.”

“I know, but tell them that.” He ran his hands through his light brown hair. “All my life, I’d felt a pull into the medical field. When I was a kid playing soccer and someone got hurt, I sat on the sidelines with them, nursing them back to health, so-to-speak.” He suppressed a grin as his eyes got a faraway look in them. “In school, biology and chemistry were my best subjects, high honours in both. Whenever anyone was in the hospital, I asked far too many intrusive questions about their health and diagnosis.” With that, his chuckle fell out, and he kicked an invisible pebble on the ground.

“You wanted to change the world. I get that.”

“Not the world, just the world for that person. If I could make them feel better, that was all I wanted. I had no desire to fight the injustices in the world, that’s what my family does. Something deep inside told me I had a different purpose in life; the need to break through and be different.”

"And your family gives you a hard time for that?"

It was subtle, but he twisted away from me. "Where are you parked?"

I pulled my phone from my purse and gripped it tightly in one hand, while I discreetly fanned my keys between my fingers of the other hand. "Parkade." I tipped my head in the general direction.

"Come on, I'll walk you to your car."

"Honestly, I'm okay. It's not that far away." There was a security guard on patrol not fifty feet from where we stood, walking towards us.

"Humour me."

It was hard to say no to the sweet smirk on his face, plus it was the safer of two options; he could walk with me or I could race-walk to my car alone. "Fine." I spun towards the parkade. "Where are you parked?"

"Just behind it, on the main road."

Perfect, then it wouldn't be a far walk for him after he'd escorted me. Although I'd made the journey to my car alone several times, there was something comforting about having a strong man walking with me. And damn it, if it wasn't starting to unravel me.

Chapter Six

Sunday, June 14th

Another day spent hanging out in the lab. Weekends were my prime time as there was usually no one in there, at least not in my area of the lab. I cherished the time, quiet and aside from the three-hour reminders, being virtually undisturbed.

Today I'd isolated my mother's gene; the one that contained all the building blocks for the construction of her pancreas, and mirrored that on my own gene. Of course, there were going to be a lot of differences as I inherited a set of genes from my father, but it was all I had to go on. Perhaps I could see the subtle differences in the mating of the base pairs that made me different and I could narrow down further the sequence that triggered the onset of her cancer. Did it develop from a mutation? Or was it like an infection, and one bad cell infected another and then split? It was a question I was going to get to the bottom of.

Hopefully. Even if there were a thousand different genes to go through. It was personal and I planned on being thorough.

The marvelous beauty of a gene stared up at me through the twin eyepieces of the electron microscope – I was seeing a part of my mother I doubt many, if any, had seen. Certainly, her oncologist hadn't looked at her cancer from a molecular level.

I was so excited by what I was seeing, I took many digital pictures to study later and compare. Marking the files one by one, I saved a copy to my personal drive, and backed up everything onto a zip drive, which I safely tucked into a zippered compartment in my purse when I locked up the lab. It had been a great day and I was ready to kick back and unwind.

I wondered what Theo was up to and found myself absently dialling his number. He'd been excited at what I'd been working on yesterday, and hearing his excitement in my work just made it more thrilling. My colleagues would've just swept it under the rug because there'd been no actual discovery. So, goal orientated sometimes. Where was the joy in seeing the beauty in something?

"Hello?"

"Hey, Theo. It's Izabella." I bit the corner of my lip to stop myself from squealing with joy.

"Ah, the lady of the lab. How's it going?"

"Well…" And so much for keeping myself contained; I launched into my day's work.

"That's amazing."

"Thanks. I knew if anyone would be excited, it would be you." My smile was canyon wide. "I'm getting hungry and wondered if I could treat you to supper? As friends," I added for clarification. "Just like colleagues."

There was a slight hesitation. "Umm, sure. Give me a few minutes to finish up what I'm working on here. Where can I meet you?"

"I've always wanted to try that new place on Whyte." I rattled off the rough address. It was only a few blocks from both the lab and my place.

"I know it, it's a great place. My friend owns it."

"Excellent. Meet you there in an hour?"

After agreeing, Theo hung up and I raced home, quickly tossing off my scrubs and lab wear and pulling on a cute pair of shorts and a floral blouse; something that made me look less like a scientist and more like a lady. I even slipped into a pair of flats. I re-pinned my hair into a messy knot, but one that looked perfect for a summer night.

Amazingly enough, I walked to the entrance of the restaurant in record time, even donning a latex glove to collect three pieces of garbage on my way. Why were people so inconsiderate? The waste receptacle was five feet away.

The local strip on Whyte Avenue was famous for terrible parking but well known for the must-visit locales. The trendiest of all places seemed to pop up on this street and Nobelle's was no different. The owners, apparently a friend of Theo's, bought the old rustic-looking corner shop and renovated it. Now it maintained its rustic look, which was making a comeback, but it also had a roof top patio. Something we Edmontonians, with our long winters, all enjoyed.

I spotted Theo rounding the corner before he saw me. He looked fresh in his shorts and tee, sporting aviator shades that gave Maverick a run for his money. Theo's hair was shiny and reflected particles of sunshine as if he'd just stepped out of the shower. Hot day-um!

He gave me a nod when he locked eyes with me. "Good evening."

"Hey," I breathed. There was a hint of cologne coming off him, something sultry and spicy. It was all at once appealing and intoxicating. "You look nice."

"As do you. Did you wear that to the lab?"

I laughed. "No. I changed. Long pants are a requirement."

"Makes sense." He pointed to the entrance. "Shall we?"

I nodded and walked ahead of him into the restaurant, where my ears were treated to soft jazz music. Based on the exterior, I thought rock music or even elevator music would be playing so the jazz was a complete surprise. But the deeper in we went, the more fitting it was. The interior was dark and moody, very much like the jazz club the girls and I went to a while back. I half expected to see a stage in the corner.

Theo walked up to the hostess station. "Two please. And Garrett is expecting us."

"Ah, yes. Theo, right?"

My non-friend-colleague-only supper date nodded.

"Garrett has you on the roof, is that okay?" She grabbed two menus and wrote on the podium.

Theo glanced at me. "Does that work?"

"Sure, I'd love to sit up there." It wasn't so hot outside today that it would be uncomfortable.

"This way, please."

We headed up a long flight of stairs on the side of the restaurant and entered a rooftop patio like something out of a travel magazine. A quick turn around the corner and we were treated to a view of the strip which at night would be quite spectacular with all the lights hanging over the road between the shops and restaurants and bars. In the daylight however, it was okay. Giant umbrellas provided shade, and there were outdoor patio sets of cushioned couches and chairs, rather than the standard table and chairs. It really gave the rooftop patio a very relaxed outdoor vibe, especially with the beach music playing on the speakers. It was a completely different place than downstairs where we came in.

"Nice, eh?" Theo said as the hostess sat us at a cozy spot with two wicker style loveseats and a low table between us. We were tucked off to the side, my over-sized chair backed against the glass railing, overlooking the strip.

"This extends if you'd like more of a table while you eat." She gave me a quick demonstration and pulled up a section. And with a quick flick, the tray collapsed back into the table. "Your server will be right with you."

"Thank you," Theo said and leaned back into his spot. "What'll you have to drink?"

"I'm good with water." I hadn't even touched the drink menu between us.

"Really?"

"Water's better." I winked. "And studies have shown fewer shenanigans happen after water consumption."

A broad smile leaked out of him. "I suppose that much is true. Hope you won't think less of me, but I'm having a beer."

"Power to you."

"Are you not a big drinker in general? Or just not since that trip?"

I shook my head. "I rarely touch the stuff, except it seemed in Vegas where I indulged a little too much." Plus, my bestie Camille was learning to control her drinking, so for the most part, Tess and I stayed dry to encourage her, as did her boyfriend.

Theo tapped the drink menu, breaking me out of my thoughts. "They were good drinks, weren't they?"

"What? Oh yeah. That pink drink in the long bottle we picked up at the Stratosphere was amazing."

It had been a hot November day, the weekend before the US Thanksgiving. Theo, myself and a group of others had dared each other to ride one of the rides at the top of the Stratosphere. I managed all three, believing all the adrenaline in my system would've burnt off the alcohol I was pounding back. It failed. Miserably.

"Not as good as the drink they lit on fire at the Mirage." Theo mock ignited a tall imaginary drink.

"That was a good one too." So many drinks, in so short a time. Kind of amazing I didn't get liver damage from the overindulgences I partook in. "It was quite the hangover the next day."

He clasped his hand to his forehead. "Don't make me remember. I thought I was going to die. I've never made friends with a toilet before."

I laughed, recalling my own pain. "I think if I'd puked, I would've felt better. Instead I had to deal with the worst headache I've ever experienced. And the dehydration. I seriously worried I'd end up needing an IV to help with that."

"It took me three days until I felt normal again. All my tried and true remedies failed."

My eyes widened. "Me too. Catching a plane ride that afternoon was hell."

"It's too bad we didn't stay in contact with each other."

Perhaps. He seemed like a decent guy, easy to talk to, easy on the eyes, shared similar interests. But it was better this way. In a couple of weeks, we'd be officially unmarried to each other and able to go our separate ways. There was no way I could be attached to anybody right now. Once the whole annulment situation was dealt with, I was going to be the head of a company I knew very little about, and would need to sink myself into learning it all. My lab time would be reduced to work hours only, if that.

Oh god. Was I going to have to take a leave from work to focus on Merryweather-Weston? That thought hadn't occurred until now. There was no way I'd be able to do both. Not successfully. And I owed it to Grandpa to get it all handled first. Damn it. Yeah, after the court meeting, my joke of a social life was going to get a serious overhaul. Bigtime. There would be no time to see anyone, not even my friends. Sadness filled my soul and I shrugged to Theo's wish of having stayed in contact.

"You disagree?" A look of rejection flittered across his face for a brief moment.

"It's not that I disagree, it's that the timing really sucks. My life is uber-complicated." And it got more complicated by the minute.

"Well, you are trying to find a cure for cancer and avenge your mother's death."

That made me smile because it sounded like I was a female version of Inigo Montoya. "I'm not trying to avenge it, per se. Yes, she was taken way too early but if I can prevent others from going through that, then something positive will have come from her passing. Kind of like you, trying to make a difference for one person."

"How long has it been?"

"Since her death?" I inhaled and slowly released my breath when he nodded. "Four years."

"Wow, that's rough."

"I won't lie. It really was at first. But my grandfather was my rock. She was his daughter, after all, and we needed to lean on each other a lot those first few months."

"That's great. Family is important."

"And yet, you feel you are shunned by yours." I cocked an eyebrow.

"Not shunned. I'm just a walking disappointment. They still accept me; they're just not thrilled with my choice of career. Big difference."

I supposed there was some, maybe not a major one though. "And they are all lawyers?"

"Every single one of them. Well, just the men."

"And the women?"

"They don't work but they marry well, like my mom for example. Married my dad, produced six kids. She had no time to join the outside world. Too busy keeping us all in line."

"Wow, there are six of you?"

"Three older brothers, me and two younger sisters." There was pride in his voice.

"And your sisters? What do they do?" I couldn't imagine them being raised to only marry well and produce kids. That sounded so… sexist.

"My youngest sister is a senior in high school with no plans for post-secondary except to travel the world, and my other sister just got married last fall. To a military lawyer."

Guess Mr. Breslin senior was still stuck in the 1930s. "Sheesh." However, there was something more incredible to his life. All of his major holidays, there had to have been a large gathering of people to laugh and play with. My holidays, especially of late, were lonely occasions.

Pride continued to radiate off him. "My brothers all graduated top of their class and were highly sought after."

"Are they employed here?"

"Yep. My oldest got a job offer with a very prestigious law firm in New York City, but decided he was more of a home boy and joined my father at Breslin Law. If you ever need a lawyer…"

Oh, how I wish! Would be nice to have a connection to a decent lawyer, not that Mr. Crowe wasn't good. He was exceptional, and he had connections up the wazoo with all the best judges, but he wasn't personable. Not that it should matter, but he'd been Grandpa's lawyer probably since the company's inception. I tossed around the idea of getting fresh blood on the company's list… or would that be a conflict of interest having my former (once the annulment goes through) husband's family on board? I shuddered.

"Not a fan of lawyers?" He laughed.

"No offence to your family, but is anyone?"

"Nope. Most of them, my family excluded of course, are class A jerks."

I thought of Mr. Pratt. Yep, if ever there was a Class A jerk, he was their star student.

A young man well dressed in business casual pants and a button up, walked up to our table.

"Hey, Garrett." Theo rose and gave him a quick hug. "I'd like you to meet my friend, well not my friend really, Izabella." He gave me a weird look, not that I blamed him. What should he have called me?

I rose and extended my hand, keeping my distance respectable. I was not a hugger. "Hi."

He motioned for us to take our seats. There was plenty of room for him to have sat beside Theo, but he went to sit beside me.

Theo moved over into the space beside me, and internally, I breathed out a sigh of relief.

Garrett smiled and settled into the seat across from us. I guessed he was staying a while. "What brings you out this way? It's a long drive for you," he said to Theo.

I guess I really didn't know what part of the city he

lived in as I didn't yet have his filled-out portion of the annulment papers. Whyte Ave was only a ten-minute drive from my apartment and that was more waiting-at-lights than actual drive time, but it was easy to get to the university, which I wanted.

"Izabella. To be honest, she's never been here."

The dark-haired owner turned to me. "Well, welcome to Nobelle's." He flagged a waitress over. "Please, these are my special guests. Bring us a round of cabanas and today's special." He turned to the two of us. "You're not allergic to shellfish, are you?"

We both shook our heads.

"That'll be all for now, Serena."

Theo shuffled more to his side and stretched an arm across the top of the seat and crossed his right leg over his left, in a very relaxed manner. I envied that. Instead, I felt on edge for reasons I couldn't explain.

"So," Garrett began, "are you two some kind of couple?"

Well, damn. Talk about being direct. My eyes widened at his inquisition.

Thankfully, Theo turned to me. "Sorry. Should've warned you that Garrett is ridiculously direct." He faced his friend. "Really, you should've joined the firm."

"And give up being my own boss? No, thanks. But

back to you, my friend."

"Izabella and I are work acquaintances. She works at the lab at the UofA and we're collaborating on a project. We met back in October at a convention."

Nice save, Dr. Breslin. Ten points to you. Not to look foolish, I agreed, hoping Garrett wouldn't press and inquire about what project exactly.

"Good. After the way things went with Miss Hot Pants, you need a break from women." Garrett faced me head on. "No offence to you, Izabella."

"None taken. I'm too busy with my work to be involved."

Garrett laughed, this deep booming laugh that called attention to us. "It's better that way. We're too much work to be satisfied properly."

I wasn't sure what he meant by that, and I cast my gaze around to the street below. We were only one level up so the view was decent, and the people were easy to make out. One person caught my eye. Dressed in black and leaning against the coffee shop across the street, they held a camera. Pointed up in my direction. Narrowing my eyes, the person turned and disappeared around the corner. Busted. My heart fell with a solid thud into the pit of my stomach.

Garrett was tucked back away from the railing, so

I was sure only Theo and myself could be seen, and suddenly, my whole world flipped. If I was photographed with him and those pictures brought before the judge, would our annulment still go through? Or would this jeopardize the whole situation?

Chapter Seven

"Thanks again for tonight," I told Garrett, as we left the restaurant and exited out onto the sidewalk. Garrett had graciously comped our meal and drinks, although both Theo and I generously tipped our server.

The evening had magically transformed into twilight over the course of the evening, and the sun was slowly starting its decent into bed, even though it was after ten pm; one of the great perks of living in a city so far north of the equator. The breeze winding its way between us was a perfect combination of warmth, music pouring out the doors of nearby establishments and the smells of barbeque. Even the lights hanging over the avenue were on, adding a special something to the atmosphere.

"Are you always this quiet?" Theo stood before me as we stopped at the corner.

"I wasn't quiet."

"As soon as Garrett sat down you were."

The photographer freaked me out, but I wasn't about to share that with him. "I was just watching you and him interact. Garrett is a large personality."

Theo laughed. "Isn't he? That's why he was one of the more popular guys back in school."

I could see it. His laughter alone commandeered a legion of attraction. But his overall charm and above-average good looks would play on the heartstrings of any breathing female. Aside from me. He just didn't seem my type, as much as he tried.

"But he's a good guy."

We'd been there for four hours and there was always a plate of something we just had to try. And it was all delicious. Thankfully I nursed my one alcoholic beverage and sipped on an Earl Grey tea, otherwise I could've had a repeat of Vegas. "Yes, he is. Our bill was pricey."

"Not just with that." He turned his head away and I missed the look on his face. I wanted to know more about the person Garrett referred to as *Little Miss Hot Pants.* Had Theo and her been a serious item, and who dumped who? It was hard to tell from his expression if he had been the one to end it.

My Spidey-senses tingled again, and I glanced

around the street, looking for that camera-toting person. There were too many people crowding the corners, waiting for the lights to change, and that it made it difficult to see.

"Have you ever been to the End of the World?" He stuck his arm out preventing me from stepping onto the road.

"Is that a bar, because it's kind of late? I need to be at the lab for eight."

"And I have a full manifest of patients to see." He winked.

Touché. "Okay, I'll bite. What's the End of the World?"

"Come with me." He reached for my hand to pull me along. Despite how soft and warm it was, I pulled back. "I promise I'll bring you back to your car."

I glanced around again and saw nothing out of place. Now I was becoming paranoid. Perfect. Turning back to the sweet face of Theo's, I gave him a gentle nod. "Okay. As long as we're not too long."

"We won't be. It's not far."

Curiosity fueled me, and I walked beside Theo across the street, to a parking pad tucked off the main drag. He clicked his key fob twice and the headlights flashed on a slick, black Camaro.

"Nice ride." I admired the reflection off the paint.

"Thanks." A shy smile sported across his face. "It was a high school graduation gift from my father."

I nodded, impressed. Not that I could complain. My grandfather and mom gifted me with an all-expenses paid, six-week backpacking trip through Europe for my high school graduation.

He held the door for me as I slipped into the slick interior, not knowing the difference between vinyl and leather.

On the quick five-minute ride, Theo waxed poetically about how all his siblings received a brand-new car at graduation. His older siblings had begged for the higher end cars—BMWs and Mercedes—but all he wanted was a good ole Chevy Camaro, so his father doled out money for a fully loaded ride. Admittedly, it was a nice car, much nicer than my Volkswagen.

Theo parked along a side of road. "We're here."

I opened up my door before he could and stepped out. Huge houses, in weird boxy shapes, sat across the road, and the other side was a forest of tall trees, leaves dancing in the gentle breeze. "This is the end of the road?" From the looks of things, he could drive in either direction. There didn't seem to be an end in sight, unless it was around the corner.

"The end of the world," he corrected. "We need to

walk a little to see it."

Both our eyes fell to my footwear. Good thing I had the sense to wear flats and not the heels I had contemplated. "Lead the way."

It was a short stroll on a paved sidewalk, past a couple of the enormous homes. A path presented itself, nestled between towering elms. At the end of the brief sidewalk a staircase descended the embankment of the river and ended at a fenced off viewpoint.

"Oh wow," I breathed out as I took in the view from the top of the stairs. The sun was setting, bathing the river and the valley in gorgeous hues of ambers and oranges.

"It's better further down."

There weren't as many stairs as it seemed, maybe fifty, but once we got to the platform, an eerie silence settled around us. At the top of the stairs, it was like a walk in a neighbourhood with cars driving by, the odd dog barking and a general murmur in the air, but down here? All that I heard was the rustle of leaves, and nothing else. I shivered, but not from the cold.

"You okay?"

I leaned closer to him. "It's so quiet." My voice fell out in a whisper, I couldn't help myself. We were all alone too.

"Indeed, it is."

"What are we looking at, do you know?" Nothing seemed familiar, at least not from this vantage point. Google maps may shed some light.

"Of course. Across the river is the Whitemud Equine Centre and the zoo." He pointed to the far right. "Over there is Hawrelak Park. See the top of the tent?"

I scanned the horizon in the fading glow of daylight, trying to find it. That tent should've been easy to spot. It was white and stretched higher than the treetops. It took a minute, but I did see the peak of it. "Yep." My voice was still low, but so had Theo's been. "Why do they call this the end of the world?" I leaned over the metal railing to look beneath me. Trees and shrubs were in abundance, but definitely no road.

"A long time ago, Keillor road used to run along the south side of the river and joined with Saskatchewan Drive where we parked, but soil erosion took the road away and the city closed it down. Up until a year ago, you could only get here via a narrow and dangerous path. But you could sit on those pillars and enjoy the view." He pointed beneath us and I craned my head overtop to see what he was talking about. Indeed, there were four pillars and a thin concrete beam.

"Did you ever?"

That sheepish smile creeping across his face said it all.

"You daredevil."

"Maybe. I like taking chances on things that scare me." He faced the setting sun; the soft light painted him in a flattering colour. It made him appear more tanned that he was, but it was mesmerizing, and I couldn't take my view off him and over to the main attraction. "You know the sunset is that way?" A voice as sweet as Grandma's homemade apple pie broke through to me.

I cleared my throat and thanked the reddening colours in the sky for washing me in their softening hues. Maybe he couldn't tell it was a maddening rush of blush that was responsible for the change.

He gently shouldered me with his arm. "I'm just giving you a hard time."

"I know." My words were as weak as my legs.

The sun dropped below the tree line across from us, and the sky magically transformed into the impending call of night with its rich magentas and indigos.

"Thanks for showing me this. It's pretty amazing."

"Have you lived here all your life?"

"Sure have." And in pretty much the same neighbourhood too. Living downtown was the best. Anything you wanted was within walking distance, and most of the time, I'd bike to work. I rarely drove, except when I knew I'd be working late in the lab, but I was smart enough to not bike home after dark. Bad things happened in the pitch of night.

And thinking of how the viewpoint was starting to fall under the night sky and there were no streetlights down here, my gaze darted between the trees, and my ears stretched out to hear the bad things before the bad things could find me. With my heart pounding, I walked over to the base of the stairs and looked up, scanning the area. I faked a yawn and covered my mouth. "I should probably get home. Would you mind taking me back to my car?"

Theo stood beside me at the base of the stairs. "Not at all."

A scuffling sound, like runners on gravel, followed by the sound of small rocks rolling down an embankment made me jump towards the middle of the stairs.

"It was probably a squirrel."

Sure, squirrels in this part of the world were known for being a hundred pounds or more.

Theo gave me a curious look. "Maybe a dog? But there was no barking or anything."

His statement fell on deaf ears. That sound came from beside us, and the drop off was quite steep. I faked another yawn. "I'm sorry. Guess I'm tireder than I thought." More tired, not tireder. Good grief, he was going to think my IQ was less than ten.

"There's nothing to worry about."

"Who's worried?" I took a couple of steps up and turned to face him. He was eye to eye with me, so close. Admitting my fear wouldn't – shouldn't – make me appear weak. "I'll be honest with you." My eyes darted around, peering through the blackness lurking behind the bushes, before I returned my focus to him. "The dark scares me."

"The dark can't hurt you."

A logical statement I've told myself several times over the years. Of course, *the dark* can't hurt me, but things hiding in the dark could. I looked deeply into his face, searching for the mocking look I expected. "I know but–"

His finger touched my lips. "You don't need to explain."

A sigh of relief fluttered through me. Thank god. I leaned to the left of his face and planted a soft kiss on his whiskery cheek. "Thank you."

He pulled back. "For what?"

"For being you."

"When I vowed whatever it was I vowed," a slight chuckle rolled out of him, "I'm sure it included keeping you safe. And that, I promise to do. It's the right thing."

With that statement, my heart shrunk without

reason. Theo was only being a gentleman in his promise to keep me safe, but for some reason, I found myself wanting more.

Chapter Eight

The short drive back to Nobelle's was quiet, as I didn't want to open my mouth and say anything to ruin the magic of the time we'd spent together. Putting my foot into my mouth was a sport I'd excelled in. However, Theo hadn't been exactly chatty either. Was he as weighed down by new emotions as I suddenly was?

We pulled into the parking lot behind Nobelle's.

"Which one is yours?"

"The green one." I pointed to the Volkswagen tucked close to the sidewalk. Despite it being a Sunday evening, the parking lot was rather full.

He parked behind my car so the headlights lit like a neon sign. "There you go."

"Thank you. For tonight. For being excited about my work and sharing in that joy." Something that didn't happen often enough.

"No problem. What are non-friends for?" There was a casual mocking tone to his voice, but I wasn't irritated by it. In all fairness, the parameters of our relationship hadn't really been established, but I didn't know how to respond to his statement. "Keep me updated on how things are going with your mom's genes and DNA."

"Sadly, there isn't much time during the week that I can devote to it. I have my regular research to keep abreast of." Drug trials and all that.

"Still."

"You'll be the first I call with any exciting news." I waved my phone as I exited the car.

He followed suit and stood beside his open door. "Even if it's not. I mean, you can call me, even if there isn't news to talk about it. We could always talk about medicine or burger places." There was more than a tinge of hope coming from him.

It was true; the evening had been fun and spontaneous, and he was great company. We had more in common than I first believed. Instinctively, I nodded. "Sure." A smile replaced any apprehension I had. Deep down I could handle a friendship with him. He could be like one of my colleagues, although none of them ever made my heart pitter-patter at seeing them, and I never felt as comfortable with them either. This was uncharted territory for me. How to keep my distance from the guy I'm married to, until our annulment goes through?

I walked over to my car and opened the door, giving the interior a quick scan. All safe. Leaning against my beater, I tried to be as casual as I could, even though tonight had been more of a date night than I'd had in recent months. "Thanks again for tonight."

Theo bridged the distance between us. "It was fun, I'm not going to lie." He stood close, and if it were anyone else, I would've backed up and claimed personal space breach, but it wasn't just anyone.

I gazed up into his face.

He gazed down into mine, emotions swimming in the thick of his brown eyes. "I want to kiss you." The words were as light as the breeze.

And I wanted to be kissed, to remember what those lips felt like on mine. It had happened once or twice in Vegas, but being so drunk, my memory on the sensations was fuzzy.

He pushed my wispy hair off my shoulder, and I allowed his hand to linger there, loving the way it felt so natural. Slowly, he tipped his head to the side and leaned toward me. Our lips barely touched as his hand caressed my arm.

"Get a room," some asshole yelled out from the sidewalk.

I pulled back, shaking my head. What the hell was happening? "I'm sorry. I need to go." It pained me to not make eye contact, but ironically the yelling jerk had saved me, and I needed to follow logic. This was not the time to go and allow my heart to lead. There was too much at stake and I needed to make sure my grandfather's business remained in the family.

Theo waited until I closed my door and started the engine before he walked away. I was an evil person for leading him to believe there was a promise of more, even if I had warned him there never could be.

# # #

No matter how much I tried, I couldn't get that hurt on Theo's face to leave my mind. All through Monday's work, and at the most inappropriate times, suddenly an image of those sexy eyes that spoke volumes, the thick, light brown hair, the facial stubble, that body I wished I could put to good use, they all put me to distraction.

I stepped off the elevator onto the 39th floor where the plush carpeting and marble countertops screamed 'we over-charge our clients' and stopped at the front desk.

"Hi, Miss Richardson."

Being a high-profile client came with perks. Sadly, not the kind I enjoyed, such as being known. "Good afternoon, Tina."

"Mr. Crowe is still working on your request. If you have a seat, I'll let him know you've arrived."

"Thank you." I scooped my dress under me and sat on the oversized plum-coloured sofa. The whole waiting room, if it could even be called that, was designed to put people on the edge; oversized chairs that made you feel small, oil paintings of the founders with eyes that seemed to stare and follow you around, and little mugs of espresso beside a machine that belonged in a coffee shop, not a lawyer's waiting room.

How did Grandpa decide that Morgenstein, Greenback and Filarski were the best lawyers to handle his company? Their business relationship went back years, well before I ever came along, but had he even wanted to change? It was probably one small piece of the ginormous puzzle I was on the verge of inheriting. Full ownership was within my grasp, and from there, I could do with it whatever I wanted. There was still the whole issue of deciding what that was to be. I needed help. Major help. And calling the lawyer's today was the first in what would be a laundry list of phone calls.

"Miss Richardson?" The receptionist walked over to me. "Mr. Crowe is ready for you. He'll meet you in boardroom three. Allow me to walk you there."

I rose and followed her down the hall, well aware of where that boardroom was. That was the room where Mr. Pratt had handed me my future from my past.

Deep laughter bounced out the opening door. "Thanks for the tip. I'll see you and Margaret on Friday night." Mr. Pratt stepped out from the boardroom into the hallway.

Unable to retreat into any other space, I remained visible where he eyed me up and down like a piece of meat. "Miss Richardson, what a pleasure to see you." He pounced toward me.

"The pleasure's all mine." My most professional smile graced my face and I extended my hand in greeting. "I trust you're having a pleasant day?" Kill 'em with kindness, that's what my mom always said.

"It just keeps getting better." A Cheshire Cat grin spread from ear to ear.

"That's great."

The receptionist stopped at the entrance to the boardroom and pointed inward, like a game show hostess highlighting today's big deal.

"Enjoy your evening, Mr. Pratt."

“You too, Miss Richardson.” He sauntered by me, the weight of his footsteps barely absorbed by the plush carpeting.

“Thanks, Tina.” I squared my shoulders and lifted my chin as I entered the lion’s den.

She left and closed the door behind her.

I walked over to the long, mahogany table and shook Mr. Crowe’s hand, surprised to see a file box with my name on it out in the open. Especially after Mr. Pratt’s was present. Wanting to give the company lawyer the benefit of the doubt, I tucked my suspicions into my back pocket.

“Good evening, Miss Richardson.”

“I see you have my request ready.”

“Yes, ma’am. My secretary has graciously copied all the files on Merryweather-Weston from the last ten years, including all records of board meetings, financial statements, and any other information deemed pertinent.” He tapped the top of the box.

And it was all in one box?

I pulled the box across the table and lifted the lid. His secretary, whom I assumed did all the grunt work, had neatly labeled and organized the files. It probably took the better part of a day. I eyed Mr. Crowe, trying like hell to keep my suspicions under wrap. “And it’s all in this one box?" Given the amount of information, I expected there to be dozens of boxes.

"There are also two more on the floor." With a grunt, he hoisted them both onto the table.

Why were those two on the floor, out of sight, while this one with the financial statements sat on the table in Mr. Pratt's presence? "And a list of the accounting officers used is also included?"

"Anything we thought was pertinent, Miss Richardson."

"And what about what you didn't think was important for me to know?"

"I assure you, everything is in there." He tapped the box closest to him for good measure. "Mr. Pratt gave his approval for this, and-"

"What does Mr. Pratt have to do with this?"

"Miss Richardson, you are not yet a majority shareholder of the company. Until you are, Mr. Pratt is the acting President and has say over what can and can not be shared. But because you are family-"

"I am also the second in command, am I not?" I reached across the table and pulled the second box closer. "Even with half of what my grandfather left to me, that still put me as the second highest shareholder. And don't all board members, all thirteen of us now, decide on the future of the company and its policies and directions together? Without having all the information, I would be doing a disservice to Merryweather-Weston."

"With all due respect, Miss Richardson. For the last few board meetings, your absence has been noted."

"And with all due respect, I held 10%, but had read all the minutes of the meetings and had voted on all addendums and changes." But the reality had been that I knew very little about the company. There had been no reason to pay that much attention to it because Grandpa wasn't going anywhere. He was a healthy man, full of life and vigor. If that accident hadn't occurred, he'd be running this business until he was eighty or older.

Mr. Crowe sighed in frustration.

I relaxed my voice. Mr. Crowe wasn't the enemy, at least in the present moment. "I need access to the rest of the information, please. Surely as the Vice-President of the company, you can concede that to me."

"Yes, Miss Richardson. I'll have the rest of the files copied and delivered to you."

"Have them delivered to my apartment please."

Right now, I needed to know it all, even if I didn't understand most of what was in here. That was plan B. Hire someone on the outside who did, who could make sure it was correct, and could give me the Coles Notes version on how the company was run. Internally I was kicking myself for not having paid more attention at the meetings I had actually been at. Like when my mother died, although the board members graciously allowed me to grieve.

Mr. Crowe put the third box on the table. "Can I get someone to assist you with taking these down to your vehicle?"

"That would be most helpful. Thank you."

Mr. Crowe lifted the receiver on the phone. "Tina, have Johnson come and assist one of my clients in moving some boxes." He settled the cradle back into the phone. "Help will arrive shortly." He pushed one box at a time across the table.

A young man who could've been an intern, arrived within a minute. "Yes, sir?"

"Please help Miss Richardson to her vehicle with these."

"No problem, sir."

Testing the weight of each box, I grabbed the heaviest, allowing the kid to grab the two lighter ones. With a grunt, he followed me down to my car and helped me load them in. "I expect the other boxes tomorrow."

###

Twenty minutes and three trips up the back stairs from the parking lot later, I had the boxes in my apartment. I still didn't know what to do with them, but it was a start. I supposed I could go through the financials and made sure everything lined up, however, staring at the first file with the most recent taxation year, my head began to swim. I was clearly out of my league. Plan B was about to be quickly instated – I needed help. Shit.

Chapter Nine

Tuesday, June 16th

The reasons for not calling another lawyer were long. I had no idea who to trust and thought I'd need a separate lawyer to draw up a non-disclosure contract, so that I could then approach another lawyer to see if everything was on the up and up. Grandpa got into this much easier than I was dumped into it, since he started it from the ground up and the company had grown with him. And mom? When she went off to college, the company was a small fraction of the size it is now. Over the past ten years, there'd been a doubling of stores every two to three years.

Grandpa had been both the President and the CEO of Merryweather-Weston. His Chief Financial Officer was Mr. Pratt, who was also, for temporary reasons only, now the President. I would need to find out if this was a conflict of interest or not, him holding both positions.

If I succeeded in getting the annulment, I'd become the President of the company, the majority shareholder, but I would have no official title other than that. I was not one of the directors running the company, thankfully. The second box had the list of all those employees, all forty-six of them. I was also not one of the appointed officers who carried out the day-to-day business aspects under direction of the directors. When I got the annulment, I would be the greenest President ever to own a company. What was desperately needed was a new CEO.

However, I imagined that that position was already filled, and would've been within days of Grandpa's death. I flipped through a few more files looking for that information. It was all so confusing and headache inducing.

I slumped onto my sofa and rubbed my temples. Maybe it was better if the company was run by Mr. Pratt. After all, he'd been in third in line, after Grandpa and Mom.

Wait a minute. What happened to Mom's shares when she'd died? I knew for a fact that I didn't get them. My shares remained unchanged.

I searched through the three new boxes that FedEx had dropped off earlier and rifled through more files, not 100% sure of what I was looking for. Something with her name on it. A will or trust or agreement that said what to do with her shares. File after file I searched and found nothing.

My kitchen table had turned into a tiny boardroom, and files were stacked on chairs, the microwave stand and just about any flat surface. Yellow stickies marked the files with a quick idea of what I thought each contained. But I'd yet to find anything on my mom, and she was pertinent information. Her shares could be a valuable asset for me to have and would be a marriage saver. If I had her share – which if memory served me correctly, were in the twenty percentile range – even with half of my inherited shares, I'd have majority, and I wouldn't have to give up the marriage either. It would be a win-win.

Nothing.

Box after box and more piles created, and still I came up empty handed. Where was Mom's Last Will and Testament? Surely the company had that on file as her shares would've been transferred to someone.

Deep, hungry suspicions welled up inside, and I hated feeling like that. I wondered if someone had 'forgotten' to copy that. Surely Mom would've had a copy. I was going to need to grab her boxes from storage and search through those. Someone somewhere had a copy, if not the original, and it most definitely wasn't me.

A knock came from my door, and I dropped the file marked "Acquisitions" onto the table. It landed with a thud and knocked over a stack of files. In a slow-motion event, the files started sliding, their destination the floor. One by one, the files hit, some on the corners, but all spilling their contents in a mishmash of mixed up papers.

"Shit," I borderline yelled, waving my hands in the air. "Just a second." I surveyed the paper pile up and figured it was best to leave it, hoping there was at least a semblance of order to putting it all back together again. "I'm coming, Mrs. Grabbenstein." I didn't even peek through the peep hole before opening. "Oh, hey."

Theo stood on the other side, half his face hidden behind a bouquet of flowers.

I cocked my eyebrow. "You know, you're really supposed to be buzzed in." But I smiled as I said it.

"But then you truly miss out on the element of surprise." He pushed the ribbon-wrapped flowers toward me. "For you."

I breathed in the sweet smell of carnations and lilies. "Thank you, they're lovely." Wonder what brought this on?

"Am I interrupting anything?"

My eyes left the gorgeous hues of sea blue, peach and yellow, and flew over to the stack of white papers with the occasional camo green and beige file folders mixed in at the other end of the kitchen. “Not really.”

A soft sigh blew out of me. All that lay ahead of me now was hours of reorganization.

Theo walked in and closed the door behind him. “I feel bad for the other night. For kissing you, especially when you’d asked me to not even be your friend.”

“Don’t feel bad about the kiss, that was all on me.” Grabbing a vase from the top shelf, I filled it with water and added the flowers. A better spot was needed to fully appreciate the unexpected gift, so I walked into my cluttered living room and put them on top of the coffee table, pushing a couple of folders off to the side.

“Big project?” Theo gazed all around.

“You could say that.” It looked like a paper factory had thrown up in my place.

“Anything I can help with?”

“Not yet.” Before I said anything further, I closed my mouth. “So, what brings you over to this side of town.” My gaze lingered on a set of folders, hoping that magicall,y the ones I’d been searching for would now appear. A moment of calmness in a mountain of chaos often did that.

“Well, my apology for starters. I think you thought I was trying to force myself on you because you pulled away and left in a hurry."

"I never thought you were forcing yourself on me. Me leaving in a hurry had zero to do with you."

"I was there. Believe me, I know I was a part."

I smiled. "Fine, I'll concede. But just. My feelings are mine, and I have reasons for not sharing or explaining."

He eyed me, almost like he was trying to figure me out, which I'd been told from other men, was impossible. I was okay with being complicated, as it helped me sort through those who had a true reason for being in my life versus those who just wanted a piece of me or the family money I never touched.

"Fair enough," he said, running his fingers through his hair. "I just want you to know that I would never–"

"And I didn't think that. Just put your mind at ease, please." I picked up a few folders and cleared a section of couch for him. "Have a seat."

He sat down, crossing his leg, and I cleared off more folders, setting the pile near the TV on the floor.

I sat on the arm of the other sofa. "I'm going to be honest with you, brutally honest."

He dropped his feet to the carpet and leaned forward, his expression one of concern.

"This is a really bad time for me to get involved with anyone. Even someone as nice as you are."

"Here it comes."

"I know it sounds cliché, but it really is me, not you. That's why I pulled away. I just can't get involved. With anyone." Too much was at stake. "If we were to wait, even a month from now, things could be different." So different. "Although, three to six months, maybe even a year would be better." There's no telling how long it would take for me to get used to being the top dog of a large company. "But right now, I need the annulment."

His eyes narrowed and his lips formed a solid line. "What's going on in your life that means you'd need to postpone a relationship?"

"I can't say."

"Can't? Or won't?"

Both, but I kept my lips sealed. How I wish our initial meeting hadn't yet happened.

"As your husband, I can help–" So much sincerity in his voice, it almost made me cave.

"Truth be told, you being married to me is part of the problem."

"Why? Why is this annulment so important?" He challenged me to a stare down, and I lost, dropping my gaze to the carpet. "Does it have anything to do with the mountainous stacks of papers in here?"

I gazed around my living room, eyeballing one

stack after another. It didn't matter if that was the reason. "Why is it not important to you?" My words fell out slightly louder than a whisper. That should be the more pressing question. I was sure any other guy would be over the moon to have an annulment granted versus a divorce, especially when the female party was paying for it all to get handled. All the guy had to do was show up, and bam, he'd be back to being a single guy without a divorce attached to him. I was truly saving the guy a lot of work in the end. And I was saving him from ever having to deal with someone like me.

"It is important to me, but for clearly different reasons." He leaned back into the couch and gave his stubble a rub. "No matter what I do, I can't figure you out."

"There's nothing *to* figure out. I'm not that girl, I'm not a catch. I have baggage, lots of it, and I refuse to burden another soul with it."

"No way. I'm not buying it."

"Good, because I'm not trying to sell you on it. It is what it is." I shrugged and walked into the kitchen on the hunt for something to drink. "Can I grab you anything while I'm up?" Not sure what compelled me to keep him hydrated, it would have been better off if he'd left and I could focus on the task at hand – sorting through the files and finding what I'd been looking for. The location of

Mom's shares. I walked over to the refrigerator.

"What do you have?" His voice sounded from the edge of the kitchen and, startled, my hand swung through the air. "Sorry, didn't mean to scare you."

"It's okay." I regained my breath and straightened up, opening the fridge door. "I have water, pop and tea. I need to go grocery shopping it seems." For good measure, I opened the cupboard to see what else I could offer.

He closed the fridge. "A tea would be nice, please."

"Coming up." I grabbed a couple of herbal tea bags and set them each inside a mug. It was impossible to ignore the sweet, charming smile on Theo's face as he made himself at home and located the sugar, dumping a spoonful into his mug and holding a spoonful over mine.

"I like mine without, thanks."

He nodded and tapped his temple. "Adding another 'like-about-you' to my growing list."

"Why?" The nicer word rolled out first, although I wanted to say *stalker.*

"Because on Saturday I need to show my family that I know you. Remember, it's part of the deal."

Right. I pretend to be the girlfriend, and you grant my annulment wishes. Easy-peasy. Wipe your hands clean of me.

"Shouldn't I know more about you then?"

He shrugged. "Only if you want to. I don't expect you to be a big talker. I've pegged you for more of an introvert, especially after watching you during dinner last night."

Well, he had that part right, although more like a social introvert. With strangers. Once I loosened up to people I knew, then there wasn't much to hold me back. Vegas found that out the easy way; pile a few drinks in me and I'd likely give away the secret codes for missile launches.

"I don't see you as an introvert," I said to Theo. Back in Vegas, he seemed larger than life, almost like a rock star with his ease around people and crowds. Part of the reason I was drawn to him. That and he'd been at all the same seminars. And was staying in the same hotel.

He laughed. "No. That's one name I've never been called."

The kettle shut off and I filled our mugs with scalding water and passed him his. "I see you as a party guy, maybe more so in your college days, a popular one for sure, sort of a less rowdy version of your friend Garrett." Although his personality was full of charm and grace, it would be his stunning good looks that set the heart a-flutter, drawing in the all the women.

"Yes. In university. But only for the first year.

After that, it was time to buckle down and bring the marks up. I didn't want to be saddled with a ton of debt, and knew the key was scholarships."

"Honour student, were you?"

"Dean's list."

That was quite an achievement. "Once?"

He held up his hand and produced all three fingers. Wow, he was really smart. Good thing though. I'd rather have an intelligent man for a doctor than one who barely passed med school.

"I don't go around advertising it."

I wasn't sure why he wouldn't. Smart rolled into a very well-maintained package. Any woman who found herself on his arm should consider herself lucky. In my experience, you got one or the other. Theo was a rarity; good on both the inside and outside.

He sat down on the couch and made himself comfortable, leaning back and resting his foot on his knee.

I took my rightful place across from him. "What else should I know about you? Or the wedding?"

"The wedding will be at the conference centre."

Which meant both families were wealthy, not just rich. Somewhere in the stack of papers I recalled seeing a rental of the conference centre. Grandpa had rented out one of the giant rooms for an owner's meeting, and just the rental for the space was well into the six-figures. Before catering and extras. That little gathering of pharmacy owners had cost him nearly a million dollars. And that was for a company. This wedding was bound to be off the charts in scale and scope.

"Black tie?"

"Yes. I'll be in a tux. A cocktail dress or something similar should be fine."

I had something on the low end of black tie hanging in my closet and it should be perfect. "What else?"

"She has seven bridesmaids."

My tea dribbled from my lips, and I gave them a quick wipe. "Seven?" I'd be hard pressed to find two people I'd want to stand up for me, let alone seven.

"I guess she couldn't choose." He lifted his shoulders and reached for his tea. "The wedding is at one, and the ceremony starts at five."

"In between?"

"There'll be drinks and games."

"And chatting with family?" That awkward time for guests. The mingling hours. I ran my finger around the rim of my mug.

He inched himself closer and reached for my hand. His voice dropped to an unbelievably sexy level. "Not until after five. Between the I dos and the drinks, I have something planned for us." He wiggled his eyebrows. "Wear runners."

What? With a ball gown? That would look ridiculous. However, my curiosity was piqued. What kind of fun could we have in runners at a wedding? I tipped my head to the side. "What do you have in mind?"

"It's a surprise." The grin that spread across his face warmed the depths of my soul. All the other guys filed away in my atrocious dating history, all combined, they couldn't add up to the charm radiating off Theo.

I narrowed my eyes in mock suspicion. "Hmm, not wild about surprises, but I'll roll with that. Nothing that will hurt though?"

"What kind of surprises hurt?"

"The bad kind."

He inched closer to me and wrapped a warm hand around mine, while his eyes creased a little in the corners from the weight of my admission. "I promise, it won't hurt a bit. Might even be fun. Might even be adrenaline based."

I stared into the depths of his dark brown eyes and saw nothing but the truth. Oh, why did this man have to stumble into my life? Why couldn't Grandpa have survived the crash or why did I end up going to that conference in October? It wasn't even supposed to be me who went.

And now… here I was, married to this incredibly sweet man, with my grandfather's business dangling on the line.

Chapter Ten

Wednesday, June 17th

There it was. Hanging in the back of the closet, like I'd hoped it would be. I pushed the clothes out of the way and pulled out the plum-coloured ballgown-length dress. A little dusty on the shoulders, but otherwise it would be perfect.

The last time I wore this dress, I was at the Merryweather-Weston annual fundraiser, a night of opulence and elegance, where I danced the night away with a lot of local celebrities. It was a sweet perk to knowing Grandpa; the tv and radio personalities, along with a roster of huge name athletes who were always willing to be a part of the fundraisers. The last one was in the fall, well before my drunken night in Vegas.

I dropped out of my shorts and tee and pulled the bohemian V-neck style dress on. Yes, it still fit. Not that I had expected it not too, but you just never knew. I stared at my reflection in the closet mirror. With a little makeup and my hair done, I could pull it off. I could find myself looking like a proper lady, a regal one even.

What would Theo think to see me dressed up like this? Would he think I'm someone special, and not just the drunken girl he got hitched to in Vegas?

My skin tingled picturing Theo's imagined reaction. If only. It was a pipe dream, something that will never happen. Why am I torturing myself like this? I knew full well that my life was on the cusp of a major change. Buh-bye mediocre social life. Hello board meetings and learning company policies and flying around to meet the individual owners. My infrequent free time was about to go up in smoke. Romance was going to take the backseat to anything and everything having to do with the Merryweather-Weston brand.

With the realisation of a dream vanishing, I allowed the dress to puddle on the floor while I changed back into regular clothes. The dress needed a freshening up, so it was time to run it over to the cleaners.

Not sure what time I was meeting Theo, I hunted around for my phone. It was sitting on a pile of papers I'd been going through earlier in a more detailed scan trying to figure out what happened to mom's shares.

I texted Theo, who seemed not to be a fan of

texting. My phone buzzed instantly with an incoming phone call.

"What's up?"

Just thinking about him sitting there all casual in his scrubs and stethoscope made me smile. "I was wondering what time I needed to meet you on Saturday?"

"I'm picking you up." There was a pause. "Did I forget to tell you that, or are you just refusing to let me drive?" He laughed and my heart melted.

"You forgot."

"My apologies. I'll pick you up at twelve-fifteen. Does that work?"

"And if it didn't?" I knew it would, but I wanted to give him a hard time.

"Then we'd be late, and that very thing you're trying to avoid–"

"Which is what?"

"Being the centre of attention." He cleared his throat. "If we showed up late, everyone would stare, and I know enough about you to know that would make you exceptionally uncomfortable."

That was true. "Don't worry. I'll be home before then."

"Have a hot date in the morning?"

"Yep, sure do. Hair and makeup."

"Really?" A tone best described as sarcastic rolled out of him. "You don't need to go to those lengths. It's a simple ceremony."

"And it's black tie. Every so often I don't mind getting all fancy." What girl doesn't enjoy getting all dressed up like a princess? A morning of pampering and waxing so I could play the part of a fairy-tale princess going to the ball. Except I wouldn't need to worry about meeting my Prince Charming, he'd already be on my arm. Our own version of the clock striking midnight was fast approaching.

"You still there?"

"Sorry."

"There you are." His smile was loud and clear through the phone. "What distracted you?"

"Just thinking about that night in Vegas. I think that was the last time, aside from a funeral, where I dressed up. It's high time I did, and I'm looking forward to being all dressed fancy." My hand ran over the hung-up clothes and stopped on one particular dress. I pulled it out of the closet and held it up. Maybe I should wear it? Would he remember?

Aside from the annual Merryweather-Weston Christmas ball, the last time I got dressed up for fun was back in Vegas. Theo, myself and a couple of others went out, and I donned a fairly fancy dress I'd purchased on a whim in the gift store of all places. But it was gorgeous and as the events of the day happened, it ended up being my wedding dress. It was the most incredible shade of ice blue with a button-front and plunging neckline. Totally inappropriate for a convention, but for walking the strip? I'd felt fun and flirty. Mom would've thought it was a stunning dress and probably could've worn it herself giving it a more elegant look.

"About that night…" Theo started.

"I really should've stopped drinking. I should have had more self-control. I knew better than to drink that much." I shook my head. Of all the foolish things to have done. Why couldn't I have gotten a tattoo or something? Why did I have to enter into a marriage? And with a guy as sweet as Theo? If I had a time travelling machine, I'd go back to that night and stop the wedding. If only.

"What's happened has happened. We can't change it, even if you regret it."

And there it was again. If *I* regretted it. Why didn't he feel the same way? "It's not that I regret it."

"Just that you wish it hadn't happened."

I sighed. It was something like that.

"Don't worry, the twenty-third is coming fast enough. See you at twelve-fifteen on Saturday." The conversation ended and the line went dead.

Well damn. How typical of me. Here I'd gone and ruined what was starting out as a fun and playful back-and-forth banter. Seriously, my regret list was piling up quicker than the files I needed to go through.

# # #

Hours later, well past my bedtime, I opened the last of the night's folders. So far, everything I'd read was boring and so damn dry it made my eyes hurt. The latte I'd made after supper seemed to be wearing off and I found my head bobbing every once in a while.

"One more," I kept telling myself. "One more."

The piles were starting to resemble some sort of organized system, but it was daunting seeing them stacked all over my living room floor. Yellow stickies were everywhere and my binder full of notes followed me over to the couch where I sat down and gulped down the rest of my cold, flavourless latte.

I opened the folder. This looked less like the franchise contracts I'd been staring at for hours. At least, over the course of a few hours, I'd accounted for all 372 individually owned stores. Those companies all paid hefty yearly royalties fees, after already having paid a franchise fee to Merryweather-Weston. It's part of what helped the company become the multi-million-dollar business it was.

The words swam on the page and I blinked to bring them into focus. This folder was one of the more interesting ones I'd yet to come across. Finally, after hours of searching, I'd discovered mom's Last Will and Testament.

The document was thick, and I counted fourteen pages. The first few pages were boring, but pretty straightforward. Nothing that caused me alarm. I knew about the money she'd put into trust for me that would be mine when I turned thirty. No surprise there, aside from the amount, as I'd forgotten it was that high, and with interest. Well, let's just say, money problems were never going to be an issue. But I wasn't worried about that; my original shares (before the acquisition of Grandpa's) handed me a nice little paycheck, for which I was grateful. That allowed me to work at the university in the lab for mere peanuts, but it also allowed me to do what I loved with the added bonus of financial stability.

It wasn't the trust fund or the liquidation that snapped me wide awake; it was the allocation of Nora Weston's shares that concerned me. All my life, my mom had been single, rarely having a date aside from the odd fundraiser or gala she'd attended. I never even knew the name of the man responsible for impregnating her as he abandoned her long before I was born. And I'd never really looked into my paternal line – never had any reason to. My full legal name was Izabella Weston Richardson, and the Richardson name came compliments of my mom's best friend. She didn't even want the sperm donor's name attached to me, and she didn't want me to bare her family name either. If I was going to make my way in this world, I had to do it under my own merits and hard work.

That's why in her Last Will and Testament, I wasn't given any money – it was all held in trust until I turned thirty. By then, it was assumed I'd have made some sort of start on adulting, and wouldn't be dependent on additional money.

However, glancing over her will, a date change on the last page drew my attention. It was dated a few months before her death, but after her cancer diagnosis. I'd been there when she'd filed the document with the lawyers, because I had signed as a witness, and on this version my signature was absent. In its place was a name I didn't recognise. Why had she changed it? And the better question is, why hadn't I been informed? Had Grandpa?

I scanned the document more thoroughly, losing sensation in my left leg as I sat in an awkward position. It was a fascinating read.

The Executor had been an old family friend, more toward the business side of the friendship. That hadn't been any kind of surprise. He'd presided over the distribution of mom's property and her business assets. That's what I'd found most interesting.

Her property and personal belongings had been liquidated, aside from the few things I was able to keep, and that money added to my trust. Standard. As far as her business assets went though, her shares were not handed to me, no surprise, but they weren't all returned to Grandpa either.

Something I never knew until flipping through the pages of legalese, Grandpa had been given the Power of Attorney, the person in charge of making mom's financial and legal decisions in the event she couldn't. Interestingly enough, that document was signed and dated a week before the changed will. Her state of mind had been great up until the day before her passing when her pain levels were sky high.

Something wasn't right. Why would Grandpa have Power of Attorney? Why was the Will different? And the biggest question of the night was why in hell had she bequeathed Colby Pratt a third of her shares?

Chapter Eleven

Thursday, June 18th

My half day at work. Thursdays were fun. Work in the morning and my afternoons were spent running errands, or until Grandpa died, having lunch with him at the office.

After everything I read last night, I felt myself pulled to the high-rise building. With each ding echoing in the elevator, I made my way up to the thirty-third floor. The doors opened and I stepped into the tiled reception area where the fresh scent of flowers tickled my nose.

Someone had suggested to Grandpa and staff that the lobby be a fragrance-free zone because someone might be allergic to the smell. Grandpa laughed and claimed there was an anti-allergy medication available for that and they could buy it from his store before they even stepped onto the elevator. After that, whether he felt guilty or not, the fresh flowers disappeared. It was only recently someone reinstated that it was okay to have a sensible arrangement on display.

The bouquet however was huge and impeded my view of the receptionist. I had to stand in front of her desk to be seen.

"Oh, hey, Izabella." The lady was nearing retirement and had worked for Merryweather-Weston for as long as I could remember, often escorting me down the hall to an unoccupied office or to the boardroom to wait for Mom. She also knew I wasn't a hugger and simply sat there smiling.

"Nice flowers."

"Thanks. They're from the staff. Bailey had her baby yesterday." Bailey, her oldest daughter, had been trying to have a baby for years.

"Congrats. What did she have?"

"A little boy – six pounds, nine ounces, twenty-one inches long. They called him Dorjan."

That's different.

"Can you imagine? Dorjan. I'm the grandmother to a boy with a made-up name." She shook her head and rambled on about the meaning of it, finally waving her hand through the air. "Sorry, I got carried away." She gazed at the computer screen. "Are you here to see someone?"

"No. I just wanted to wander around, sit in Grandpa's office for a minute and think."

"You go right ahead."

"Thanks." It's not like I needed permission, but it was the right thing to do.

I passed several offices I played in as a small child, and the boardroom where I used to bring my homework after school to wait for mom to finish up. I passed by the staff kitchen, where many times I'd whip up a supper of soup and grilled cheese and share it with Mom and Grandpa. Over the years, it's grown to include fancy coffee makers and panini presses, and a smart fridge to boot. It was plain in its colour scheme – white walls with dark blue trim – the same colour as the writing on the logo.

Down the hallway to the end was where Grandpa's spacious office sat, occupying the corner section of the floor. Since his passing, it remained untouched, something the board had agreed to leave for the time being. The office had the best view of the downtown area with the floor to ceiling windows, and if one craned their neck just so, they could see the pyramids of the Muttart Conservatory and the bridges spanning the river. Sunrises in the winter were a magical sight to behold from his view. It was no wonder Grandpa was always at his desk before that happened, at least in the winter. In our summers, the sun rises at 5 am and even for an early bird like he was, that was still early.

As I approached the office, the door was slightly ajar. Odd. It was usually closed and locked; I had the key ready in my hand as I neared. A voice, and a hushed one at that, could be heard coming from inside. I stopped and listened, ready to knock when I heard a break in conversation.

"It's all but done," the voice said. "No way will she be able to get her precious annulment in time."

He was talking about me? But why? Who did that voice belong to?

"Once I have official shareholder control and the board appoints me to President, we will proceed to move onto Phase Two."

I shifted and pushed my ear closer to the crack.

"Oh hey, Izabella, how's it going?"

My heart hit the floor and I stepped back. "Great, Barney, just great. Just wanted to come and see Grandpa's office again." I wrapped my hand around the doorknob and squeezed the life out of it. I wasn't a confrontational person by nature, but I sure wanted whatever answers were sitting on the other side of the door.

"Sure, absolutely. Whatever it takes to help you heal." He turned around, shuffling back down the hall.

I pushed open the door without so much as a word.

No doubt Barney's announcement gave a quick warning to Mr. Pratt. I stared him hard in the eye. No way was he going to get away with thinking he had the upper hand. "Mr. Pratt. What a surprise to find you in this office."

He rose and shuffled the assortment of papers on the desk into a file. "I was just working. It's much quieter down here."

I crossed my hands over my chest and stood there, unsure of what my next move should be. Should I say something along the lines of knowing I'd heard his conversation, or would it be best to assume he already knew that, busted as I'd been by Barney?

Mr. Pratt closed up his file and replaced the pen into the pen holder, an elegant gift Grandpa received from some hockey player back in the day. Amazingly enough, the pen still worked, just needed a refill from time to time. "I think that should do it." He wasn't moving quickly, like people normally would if they were caught sneaking around. In fact, his movements were slow and deliberate. It was unnerving. "Are you going to be here long? Can I have Jackson bring you a coffee or something?"

"I hadn't yet decided, and I'm quite capable of getting my own coffee, thank you though."

Tucking his folder into his meaty hand, he started for the door. "How's your husband these days?"

My breath caught in my chest and I fought to swallow it down. “I wouldn’t know.”

“Of course not, why would you?” He eyed me up and down enough that the lump softened with the added bile rising up my throat. “Have a good day, Izabella.”

“You too.” I closed the door the second he stepped beyond the border and walked over to the desk. Nothing seemed out of place, at least to me. Grandpa would’ve spotted it though. You could replace a stapler back on his desk in the same position and he’d know because it’d be off a hair. He was so methodical. Probably why he was a shrewd business mogul. He knew exactly what he wanted, and precisely how to get it. Unlike me. I always felt like I was swimming in the ocean with nary a boat to cling to.

I sat in his soft leather chair and reclined, wondering what my next move would be. And what was Phase Two? Nowhere had I read there being any mention of expansion or of any type of acquisitions. It was all surreal and totally out of my league. Until I’d read Mom’s Last Will and Testament, I’d been almost ready to concede defeat and just accept the shares allocated to me and Theo, and go about my merry way, just being a low-key board member. Now though, things had changed.

I picked up the phone and dialled the receptionist’s desk. “Hey, Mona, can you tell me if the last call made in this office was incoming or outgoing?"

"I'd need to check."

"Please do, and if it was outgoing, I'll need the number please." I hung up the phone and stared out the window, tossing a glance at the family portrait hanging on the wall. Taken when I was three, just before Grandma died, we're sitting in this office. Grandpa at his desk, Grandma on one side, Mom on the other and me cradled in his lap. Compared to my friends, it was a weird family picture, but it was us. We had each other. Until seven weeks ago, when I became the sole survivor of the Merryweather-Weston line.

The phone buzzed and I picked it up, scratching down the details Mona provided.

I dialled the number Colby had called, and a high-pitched voice answered. "Good afternoon, Smith Quinn Divestitures Group. How may I direct your call?" Immediately I hung up, and on my phone typed in the name of the company. I scanned the landing page and my eyes got bigger and bigger the more I read. "Like hell."

Now more than ever, I needed the annulment. I needed share majority and to appoint a new CEO who would have the company's best interests at heart. Colby Pratt was not that man. He had plans to sell off the company. That's what Phase Two was.

Chapter Twelve

Saturday, June 20th

The humidity in the air was awful, especially for mid-June in this part of the world. Natasha, my hairstylist, had a bitch of a time keeping my hair curled; every curl quickly flattened itself out within minutes. She ditched her plans for beach-soft waves and instead pinned it up in a half pony and worked some sort of witchcraft to make it pretty. Admittedly, she did a beautiful job and it was definitely not over-the-top or too much, even after she applied my makeup.

I bid her adieu and scarfed down a high-protein smoothie to keep me fueled through the afternoon, and stashed a protein bar into my clutch for a wee snack. The shoulders of my dress were just slipping into place when the buzzer announcing Theo's arrival went off.

At least he had the decency to buzz this time, even though I was totally expecting him.

I didn't want to wear my runners, although no one would know thanks to the length of my plum dress, and instead opted for a pair of simple heels. They were well padded and amazingly comfy. Plus, they lifted the bottom of the skirt off the floor to a barely touching level.

Theo rapped his knuckles on the door I'd left opened for him. "Hello?"

"I'm in the living room." I was tossing my phone and a few personal items into my silver clutch.

"There you… Wow."

I wondered if he was still upset with me, but seeing his eyes widen and how he tugged at the collar on his neck, they suggested the anger was long diffused. "I look okay?" I straightened up and took in his full admiration.

"It's not fair to Theresa, my cousin. You're… wow… well, you're beautiful, Izabella."

Three words I'd never heard strung together, at least not in recent history. They had the power to make my heart flutter and my legs weaken. It meant so much to hear them, especially coming from him. "You're looking pretty dapper yourself." Hot damn. The tuxedo turned him from a regular Maverick into James Bond. The good doctor needed to check out my heart, I was having palpations trying not to stare at him.

He bowed. "Thank you. You're ready?"

"As I'll ever be."

We left the apartment side-by-side, and I locked up. Once we'd descended the stairs, he offered me his arm and I looped my hand through it like it was the most natural thing in the world. Together, we strode through the lobby and out the main entrance and I felt like a superstar as my neighbours turned and waved. Or maybe they didn't recognize me and questioned who I was.

Stopping at his Camaro, he opened the door and helped me in. And lifted the extra material from the bottom of my dress into the car, touching the side of my calf as he did so. Heat blossomed across my chest which was modestly covered and hopefully hid the majority of the color change. Content that none of my dress was hanging out, he closed the car door and jumped over to his side.

"Before we take off, I just wanted to say thanks. Thanks for helping me save face in front of my family."

"Even though in a couple of weeks, we'll be..." What? What was it we'll be? What do you call an annulled couple?

The chipper grin on his face fell. "Yeah, that."

It put such a sudden damper on the mood that I vowed right then and there to not bring it up in any way shape or form for the next twelve hours. After midnight though, all bets were off.

"So, where's the ceremony?" I knew the reception was at the convention center.

"In Riverdale. There's a giant church, an old historic church. My cousin is a huge Historic Edmonton fan."

"Where's Riverdale?" All I knew was that sounded like the place where Archie and Jughead lived, but I was pretty sure we weren't going into the US.

He gave me a sideways look as he pulled out into traffic. "How long have you lived in Edmonton?"

"All my life."

"You really need to see more of your city." He laughed, the sweetest, gentlest sound. "Riverdale is east of the convention centre, right on the bend of the river."

I nodded, watching my surroundings as we drove by. Maybe I did need to venture out and explore my hometown more. There were a lot of things I should do but finding the time to do them was holding me back. Between the company and trying to squeeze in afterhours time in the lab, I really had no semblance of a life.

It didn't take long until we drove into an area of the city I'd never visited. It was like something out of a movie – huge towering trees with swaying, vine-like branches hanging over the street, providing a break from the intense sunshine.

Theo parked his car behind a building and helped me out. He straightened his bowtie – twice – and his gaze darted around as other cars pulled into the parking spaces.

I wanted to tell him that I'd play my doting girlfriend role so well that he'd have a hard time imagining me not being in his life, but I also didn't want to send out any crazy mixed-up signals. He was doing me a huge favour and I didn't need to be a jerk about it. Instead, I looped my arm through his and followed his lead, putting a smile on my face and a spring in my step.

"We've got this," I whispered and tapped his chest with my other hand.

He tightened his grip, briefly, and sighed with what I hoped was relief. "There's my older brother."

I scanned the growing crowd, searching for someone who looked like he could be a brother. It wasn't hard to find an older version of Theo. Standing on the steps of the church, a man who could be a dead ringer for my date held the hand of a lovely lady dressed in pink. "Which one is he?" Theo had three older brothers.

"Ah, that's Geoffrey. His wife, the one laughing, that's Michelle."

Geoffrey and Michelle. Got it. I wasn't gifted with remembering names, but I was going to try. No better time than now.

"And there's Robert and Amanda."

I wasn't sure who he was referring to, maybe another brother, could be a friend too as I didn't see another guy who bore any resemblance to Theo.

"Come on, let's meet the family."

I swallowed down my building fear. This was all an act, and I was terrified that someone would see right through it. Did I have enough intel on Theo to legitimately pass as a girlfriend?

"Theodore," a loud booming voice said from the top of the stairs. He waltzed down as if he owned the place and wrapped Theo in a bear hug.

"Izabella, I'd like you to meet my oldest brother, Robert."

"How do you do?" I shook his hand and recited his name over in my head focusing on something about him that made him stand out – my Grandfather's trick for remembering every single one of his franchise owners. Robert Red Beard. Hopefully that would help me later.

"I'm well, thank you." His handshake was the bone-crushing variety I'd dealt with in lawyer's offices before; the kind where they crush you to let you know they have the upper hand. Did they teach that in law school?

Under the guise of my clutch, I opened and relaxed my hand to bring the blood flow back in.

“Amanda,” Robert Red Beard yelled behind him, “come and meet Theo’s girl, Izabella.”

A lovely lady, who could’ve passed for an older version of the Duchess of Cambridge, descended the steps and stood before us. “It’s a pleasure to finally meet you. Welcome to our family.” I half-expected her to curtsy. “We’re so excited to be able to put a name to the face. Theodore speaks very highly of you.”

“Does he?” I tried to hide the creeping blush by turning away and gazing up into Theo’s face. How much had he talked about me, considering he’s only known for a week about the marriage?

“Oh yes. Says you’re a gifted scientist.”

“Well,” I gave his arm another little squeeze, “I don’t know about the gifted part, but I sure do love my job.”

Amanda stepped down a stair. “Is that how you met?”

This I knew I could answer with total honesty. “Yes. We met at a pharmaceutical conference back in October.”

Theo released my hand from his arm and instead threaded his fingers through mine. “We had the absolute best time.”

“I hope we hear all about it over dinner. Are you

joining us?" Amanda directed her question at me.

I shrugged. "I'm not sure what Theo had planned. I've left the decision up to him."

"Very well. Do consider us." She tapped my arm. "If you'll excuse me." And with that she was gone.

Theo pulled me away from his brother and we walked up the stairs into the church. "We'll get bombarded if we hang out there. Just wait until dinner. You'll see."

Until Amanda mentioned dinner, I hadn't given it a whole lot of thought. I just assumed it would be some random table we'd be put at and we'd have to make small talk with strangers. Now, I'd be making conversation with his family, about how we met, how we spent our time together and whatever it was his family inquired about. I gulped, suddenly preferring awkward chit-chat about the weather with people I wouldn't need to remember later.

He pointed to a pew near the middle and guided me into the center of it. "Sorry about her, she can be quite nosey."

I laughed and looked around making sure Duchess Amanda wasn't nearby. "I hardly found her nosey at all. She seemed quite sweet. Have they been married long?"

"Twelve years?" He scratched his head. "They'd dated forever, and Robert held off proposing, claiming that he was only going to get married once and he wanted to make sure that Amanda was the right one."

"Is that a family view?"

"What the marriage part?"

"And only doing it once?"

He nodded and turned away. Double damn. So much for me keeping my promise that I wasn't going to bring up the annulment, I'd just basically rubbed back in his face that we were going to be the first to break a family tradition. He was already the different one, choosing the non-familiar law career, and now I was keeping him even more different by making him the first to have a dissolved marriage. Somehow, deep down, I highly doubted there were any divorces on the Breslin family tree so I kept my mouth firmly shut. Instead, I ran the fingers on my free hand over our joined ones.

People started filling the pews, and Theo spoke with just about every person he saw, introducing me to each of them. There was no way I was going to remember anyone's name despite Grandpa's trick, and I hoped there wouldn't be a test later. My own personal joke made me giggle.

"What's so funny?"

"Nothing." I bit my lip and asked him about his family tree.

He kept pointing out his aunts and uncles and from

which side they were on, all the way until the music started playing, at which point we both turned and watched the procession.

The wedding was lovely, and the lady beside me, whose name I forgot but was a relative to the bride, cried constantly. I nicknamed her cries-a-lot as she reminded me of a Care Bear in her fuzzy peach-coloured sweater. Halfway through the ceremony, I ended up passing her a tissue.

The bridal party made their way out of the church and we followed out to breathe in some fresh air.

"Theodore," a high-pitched voice squeaked out from behind us. She looked about high school age and ran over and hugged Theo, who returned the hug.

"Izabella, this is my baby sister Natalie."

Natalie immediately wrapped her arms around me, and I took a step back to brace myself from the unexpected. "So happy to meet you." She pulled herself off me and beamed up at her big brother. "Mom said not to leave yet. One of the photographers is willing to take a family photo since it's been a while. Come on, she's setting up in the courtyard."

"Okay, but it has to be quick. I have something planned for Izabella before the dinner."

"Promise." Natalie pulled on my hand. "You too." She led us around the church to the most gorgeous courtyard I'd ever seen. The flowers were in full bloom and the colours were a pale comparison to the most intoxicating floral scent floating in the air. Natalie walked us over to a cobble stone area, where chairs were already being set up, and various members of the Breslin family were hanging around chatting animatedly.

Theo lifted his finger as he approached the woman I assumed was his mother. "Only one picture, Mom, okay?"

"Yes, dear. One." She nodded and turned her full attention to me. "You must be Izabella?"

"Yes, ma'am." I nodded and felt like I should bow to the woman. Her eyes narrowed ever so, and I felt like she could see right through me and my pretend relationship.

Instead of continuing her glare, she air kissed each of my cheeks. "Welcome to the family."

It was unnerving how often I'd heard that today. I had so many questions about why they were saying that and what it all meant, but the photographer started gathering everyone together and placing them. When Mr. and Mrs. Breslin and their six children were all together, the photographer snapped a dozen photos.

"Alright, we'll need all the spouses."

Theo's brother's wives and his sister's husband stood beside their partners. I stood off to the side watching the family. They looked like royalty, so formal and yet, eye-catching. I couldn't tear my gaze away from them.

The photographer clicked a few, until Mrs. Breslin raised her hand up. "We need Izabella in here."

"Oh no." I backed up a step. "This is a family picture, and you all look so lovely."

She waved her hand. "I insist, besides you're family too."

I glanced over to Theo who wore the same shock I felt. It seemed he didn't expect that either.

"Stand beside Theodore. Please."

I gave him another glance and feeling wholly out of place, stood beside my husband and held his hand. Something deep inside told me the cat was out of the bag. Why else would they all act like I was family, if he hadn't told them we were already married?

Chapter Thirteen

With the family pictures out of the way, Theo and I were free to go and do our own thing. We walked out of the courtyard and down the street to his car, I held my clutch with two hands, rather than allow him to hold my hand. While I was beyond thrilled that we had plans for something, as it prevented us from engaging in any conversation with people I deemed strangers but who were family to Theo, I was a tad upset with the direction things had been going with his family. My thoughts kept falling back to the little things everybody said and how welcoming everyone was. It was more than just being friendly, it was weird.

"You're awfully quiet. I sense you have some questions for me," Theo said as we stopped at his car.

"I do."

"Can they wait? I promise to answer every single

one in twenty minutes."

I fell into my seat and gathered up the hem of my dress, tucking it all into the car.

A heartbeat later, we were pulling out of the parking lot and heading back toward downtown, driving along a winding road where the river lay beyond. I needed to sort through my thoughts, which were plentiful, and decide which ones were the most pressing to ask and which could wait.

Theo seemed to have turned introspective as he kept to himself while he drove through the myriad of tall buildings and headed towards the river. His grip on the steering wheel was turning his knuckles white even though his breath seemed even and calm. He never chanced a look at me, and only spoke when we arrived at a parking lot where a sign with the words *Rafter's Landing* hung.

"What's this?"

"Come on, we're going to be late."

He helped me out and we half ran down a rounding path. As we turned on the bend, a huge boat with the words *Edmonton Queen* painted on the side blew its horn.

"Final boarding," someone yelled out.

"Wait," Theo called, and let go of my hand to produce his phone. "I have two tickets."

"You almost missed out, son." The grandfatherly

man scanned Theo's phone and allowed us to walk onto the paddle boat.

"What are we doing here?"

"You'll see." He held my hand, and like he'd been on here a million times, he led me through the interior and over to a flight of stairs. As we ascended, the boat rattled, and I paused. "Gang plank going up."

Two more stairs and I stood on the top of the boat, the river valley all around us. "Wow."

"Just wait." He pushed through a small crowd of people and took me over to a table on the port side; it was on the river side of the boat and at this moment, had an impressive view of downtown. "For you." He pulled out my chair and I sat down, allowing the full length of my dress to drape over my feet. "We're here for an hour and a half cruise down the North Saskatchewan. I figured this would be a nice place to talk without being distracted." He glanced around. "Or the perfect place for you to ask me all the questions I see behind those beautiful eyes of yours."

The river boat was romantic and the view second to none, hardly the place to have a deep, meaningful conversation.

"So, what's on your mind?" He folded his hands together and leaned on his forearms.

I breathed out a long-winded breath. "I don't even

know where to begin. I have so many questions."

"The most important one being?" He gave me his undivided attention even as a small rush of people headed to the front of the boat to recreate a less than cinematic reproduction of the iconic moment in the *Titanic*. It was hard to be the King of the World on a small paddleboat.

In a deep continuance of avoiding answering the question, I stared beyond the crowd and took in the lush greenery on the sides of the river. The boat moved as it was released from the dock and the sounds of the paddlewheels slapping the river hummed in the air. A slight breeze washed over the top of the boat as we slowly inched our way down the river. It was more of a soothing motion and not the jarring one I'd expected.

"Izabella?" I turned my attention to him. "You can ask me anything, and I promise to answer. Truthfully." He reached across the little bistro table and held my fingers.

The words fell out of me along with a heavy sigh. "Do they know? About the marriage in Vegas?"

Time seemed to stand still and the people on the upper deck around us froze before they could take a seat at the many tables and benches. Everything moved as if in slow-motion. Even the nod of Theo's head seemed to take a while.

"Oh my god." The air rushed out of me and I

braced my head in my hands as my world started spinning. "I think I'm going to pass out."

In a heartbeat, he was in front of me. "Lean over your legs and breathe nice and slow." He squatted before me and held my face in his hands. "Just in and out." Cool air found the heated spot on my cheek when his hand vacated it and sat on my shoulder, his thumb gently rubbing the skin there.

I inhaled and reclaimed control over my body. Never in my life had I fainted, and I wasn't about it to do it here either. I also wasn't willing to be part of a scene. "I'm okay now, thanks." I rolled myself up back into a sitting position.

"You sure? You're very pale."

After a quick reassuring nod, Theo stood and slid his chair over beside mine. "I'm sorry."

"They all know?" How could he share that? Aside from the lawyers and Mr. Pratt, no one I knew, knew the truth, although I'd like to think Mom and Grandpa and Grandma knew. I'd refrained from telling my best friends, even if they'd end up celebrating the news and not chastising me. Both had been bitten by the love bug and they were eager for me to join their club of giddiness and exciting moments and planning for a possible marital future. But my story was on a whole different level than theirs, I was already married and working my way backwards to singlehood. Hardly worth celebrating, or sharing for that matter.

"At first, it was just my dad. I needed to know what my options were, after I showed him the papers you'd given me." Those dark eyes of his searched across my face. "I had him read them over just to make sure everything was legit."

The air around me cooled and I shivered but it had nothing to do with us being in the shade and moving over the river.

Theo stood and shook himself out of his suit jacket and draped it over my shoulders. "Forgive my lack of manners."

"It's okay." I pulled the lapels over my chest.

"For telling my dad?" There was a tinge of a smile brewing on the left side of his lips.

It was enough to make me crack one of my own, but only for a heartbeat. "And what did he say about your options?"

"Well, firstly that we have a good, decent judge and that your lawyer must've pulled a few strings to get us before her."

Yes, I remembered how Mr. Crowe had said he'd made a few phone calls and secured one of the best judges in the city. "I'm not surprised, it takes a good lawyer to know another."

"Then Dad asked all sorts of questions about where my head had been that night to have gone off and done something so stupid, and to have dragged you into it."

I curled myself under the weight of Theo's suit jacket, a light scent of cologne tickling my senses and ironically making me relax when I wanted to pace. I was as much to blame as Theo was.

"He said it really came down to two options; either accept that I'd made a stupid mistake and to take full responsibility for it, and walk into that courtroom knowing it was over and for the rest of my life live knowing my carelessness had affected someone other than me. Or…" He inhaled sharp enough that it grabbed my attention. "I could start courting the young lady who blindly accepted the idiot she married and prove to her it wasn't a mistake, and I could make her happy."

There was no doubt in my mind which option Theo had decided to take, because he was definitely no idiot.

"But why? Why me? Why now?"

"Why you? What a silly question. You are smart and level-headed, and cautious and endearing."

"You've known me a week, Theo, I hardly think you've had time to really assess me." Besides, I wasn't any of those things. Maybe someday I'd be deemed smart when I figured out what the trigger was for pancreatic cancer, but I was most definitely not level-headed. I just hid it well.

His thumb caressed the top of my knuckles. "That's where you are wrong. You see, when a patient comes in, I have to be able to assess them in minutes, and not just with whatever physical ailment they are there for, but to be able to see beyond that. To hear the pain in their voice or see the way they are describing their hurt. Believe me, I am able to assess my patients very well." It was said with so much self-assurance, I found *him* endearing.

"But I'm not your patient."

"You're right, you're not. But I see you, and I like what I see."

My gaze roved from our joined hands, over the muscular definition of his arms and up to stare into the sweetest face I've ever been connected to. "But we can't stay married. We don't know each other. It's not right." A thousand different thoughts presented themselves in my head for all the reasons we shouldn't be together. The biggest, of course, was the flashing neon sign of Merryweather-Weston.

"So what? So we did things different than traditionally accepted. It'll be a great story to share with our kids and grandkids some day."

Oh my god, he was already talking about having a family. My head began to swim and once again I braced it between my palms.

"Head down," Theo encouraged, and rubbed my back as I rested my head on my arms. "I'm not saying that we're planning on starting a family, it was just a rhetorical comment."

If you say so. The soothing motion was heavenly, and instinctually I found myself matching my breathing to his strokes. After a couple of minutes, I lifted my head and noticed we were approaching the Walterdale bridge, a newly constructed arch bridge.

"Feeling any better?"

Things just kept getting better with each passing minute. The annulment I wanted and had been so sure was in my grip, was starting to slip through my fingers. Between the possible sneaky photographer and Mr. Pratt's controlling shares of the company, I was now married to a man who thought our impromptu drunken wedding would make a cute story to tell the next generation.

"I need to walk." Even though I was trapped on a boat, surely I could pace off my thoughts.

"Of course." I went to shrug out of his suit jacket. "No, keep wearing it. I'm good. The sun's starting to come back out." Even though he was wearing his aviators, he shielded his eyes as he looked skyward.

Distraction. That's what I needed most. "Can we head to the front of the boat?"

"Sure."

The front wasn't very far, and it only took a few steps to reach the railing. I held on tight and leaned my forearms against the cool metal banister, watching as the murky brown water sailed by.

"Do you know where we are?"

"On the riverboat?" I let a sly grin sneak out. "I know we're seeing downtown – that's the bridge I take to the university every day."

"Do you know what those buildings are?" He pointed up the embankment to the buildings looming high with what had to be some of the best views in the city. Aside from a couple, I really had no idea what I was looking at. "May I be your travel guide?"

A smile curled up on the edges of my lips. "Sure. Dazzle me with your brilliance on this city we live and work in."

And he did. I learned more about the city in our ninety-minute boat ride than I had all throughout school. He pointed out various locations that I'd never seen from the river and wouldn't have picked out from this viewpoint. Theo had more interesting knowledge on the bridges we travelled under, and the heights of the river when it flooded years ago. I was impressed with his knowledge, and it all seemed genuine. Theo had a deep love for his city, and it showed. It's amazing what you miss even when you see it daily.

Chapter Fourteen

The Edmonton Queen began her docking procedures, but we continued to hang out on the top floor. The sun was shining and as much as I enjoyed wearing his jacket and smelling him constantly, it was time to give it back. We had a dinner to return to.

He slipped into the sleeves and I ran my hands over the shoulders to smooth it out. Feeling his strength under my fingertips was something else.

"Well, is it time to head to the reception?" A part of me was sad that our private time together was over, and it was back to reality. Back to facing Theo's family and acting like we were a happily married couple. But only for a little while. I'd have to find a way to selfishly convince him that we needed that annulment. The problem was I didn't know how.

"Are you okay with going back to the wedding,

knowing that my family knows?"

I rolled the words over in my head and sighed. "I wish they didn't, but I understand why you felt you needed to share that with them."

"What did you tell your family?"

My stomach tied itself up in knots. What would my mom have said if she was around to hear? If she was, would I have even shared with her my mistake? There was no doubt in my mind that she would've been supportive in whatever decision I needed to make. My heart longed for her. To sit in her office, with the door closed to ask for her opinion, even if she wouldn't give it me. Even Grandpa's stern voice, he would've had some awesome advice. Mind you, if he hadn't passed away, I wouldn't be in this pickle. "Do we have time for a walk? I want to share with you something personal."

He lifted his hand, palm up. I placed mine on top and he folded his hand over. "Want to cross over the bridge? We can walk all the way over to the convention center."

"What about later? And your car?"

"We'll walk back and get it. Or Uber over. It's not a big deal."

I hesitated but went with it. The Uber would be the safest option, although a walk at night would be highly romantic. Not that I wanted romance. But maybe after the annulment, we could think about it.

"What's on your mind?"

"So many things." I squeezed my clutch tighter as we turned away from the parking lot and followed a paved path toward a bridge. "And I'm going to be honest with you."

"Honesty is the best policy."

"Maybe so, but it's not always the nicest."

"Why do I get the feeling I'm not going to like what's coming?"

It wasn't going to end well for either of us, and humour, even a weak attempt at it, wasn't making this easier. "This is really hard for me, this tiny little bit of opening up I'm about to share with you." We walked a bit further, climbing up the steep path leading to the pedestrian side of the bridge. "I have no one to lean on, and there's no one in my life that I depend on. And I'm not saying this so you'll have pity on me or anything like that. I've always been a strong-willed, fiercely independent person."

"I believe that about you."

The doctor's gaze was hard to tear away from, but if I was going to let him in, I needed to look at something else. "You see, all my life, there have only been three people I've depended on; my grandpa, my mom and me, and two of those people are no longer in my life. And since finding out about our marriage, I've been thrown for a loop and I have no one to confide in or ask opinions of, although neither would've given them. Both my mom and Grandpa would've said I needed to figure out what I wanted, and presenting their opinions would sway that thought process." I stopped at a point on the bridge and stared back at the Edmonton Queen, listing gently at Rafter's Landing.

Theo remained close, never taking his gaze off me. Why was he so easy to talk to? I've already told him more in a couple of minutes than I had anyone else in a long time. I breathed out my hesitation. "Please don't think less of me, but the only people I've shared the marriage news with is my lawyer." I took a big breath and stared out into the horizon. "And he's not even my lawyer, he's the company lawyer."

"You own a company?" Even from the corner of my eye, Theo's eyes got wide.

"I'll get to that later." Oh my gosh, this was impossible. I was never going to be able to admit why I needed to be single. "My mom, she had me at seventeen, she hadn't even graduated high school yet. Grandma would bring me to the office and work while taking care of me so Mom could first finish up high school, and then go to university full time and get her business degree, which she did."

"That's an amazing family you have. Your mom was blessed, especially if your grandma was so willing to help raise you." He leaned on the railing and gently pushed against my arm.

A memory of Grandma and I twirling in the board room breezed into my mind. One of my first memories of her, I couldn't have been more than five. "She was pretty special."

"She passed away, didn't she?" He instantly hung his head.

I nodded. It was definitely a sad event, but since I was only seven, I didn't really know my grandma that well. But her loss was devastating to my mother and grandpa, and seeing that hurt on my mom's face when she spoke of Grandma, or the loss in her voice – that had always wrecked me more. "Grandma got the cancer at fifty-four and passed away."

"When you say *the* cancer, you're meaning pancreatic, like your mom?"

It was too much. Why did I think I could discuss this with him? My heart clenched at the thought of Mom going down the same road as her mom. I tugged out of his grip and slowly walked away.

Theo caught up quickly and tightened his grip around my hand as we continued over the bridge, stopping in the middle to stare towards the downtown side of the river. The buildings stood tall and proud, and in the distance I could see the tower that housed the main operations of Merryweather-Weston.

"I'm really sorry for your loss. Was your mom the same age as your grandma when she got sick?"

My gaze fell to the metal grate and a whoosh of chilly air wrapped around me. "No, no, no. She was much younger at forty-one." And if that trend continued, I was already doomed.

Theo pulled me to a stop and searched my face. "That doesn't mean you're going to get it. You could have more of your paternal genes than your maternal ones."

I nodded. "Yes, that could be true, but I doubt it." Everyone always said I was a dead ringer for my mother, in looks and part of her personality, although I'd say she was a little more tenacious than I've ever been. Probably why she was a fierce CEO. Her replacement lacked the same spirit and zest.

Theo's finger brushed across my cheek and turned me to face him. "Is that what you're worried about? That I'd fall in love with you and you could be dying in few years?"

Fall in love with me? The idea was so preposterous, I laughed. A deep laugh that only came out when I was on the verge of tears. And try as I may, the tears wouldn't stay locked away. They started to fall.

"Aw, don't cry, Izabella."

Hearing my name never sounded so beautiful. What was up with this man? How did I manage to meet with him, and really, why couldn't I have met up with him at the next fall convention when I'd hopefully have a better grasp on the business? Damn.

With a gentle touch, he wiped away the river running down my cheeks. "If you're at all concerned about the cancer, there are tests you can have done to see if you're at a predisposition for it."

"I know that."

He wrapped his arms around me, and I melted into his embrace. It felt so right, so perfect. When I looked up at him, he was gazing down upon me, a gentleness on his face and a sweetness in his eyes. Without a doubt, my body knew Theo was a one of a kind, and unlike any guy I'd even been with. In his presence, I was safe. But how did that work? We'd only known each other for a week and had only hung out those couple days in Vegas. How can the heart know in such a short time that it truly enjoyed the other person? Maybe I should switch my specialty and study that. I'd likely get my name published in the medical journals faster that way.

"You know, your honesty is far less brutal than I expected."

The comment made me smile, despite the sadness growing in my heart.

"I thought you were going to tell me that there was no way we could ever be together."

It was time to tell him. "Theo…" I pulled out of the embrace and walked a bit further towards the other side of the bridge. "This pains me to tell you, for all the reasons and details I can't share with you at this time." I inhaled sharply and focused on the handsome man before me. "I need us to get the annulment for the most selfish of reasons." I stood a little straighter and pressed my shoulders back. "For the sake of my grandfather's company, I need you and I to be not connected." My hand waved through the air, landing on the cool railing. "What I mean is, I have a meeting on the twenty-fifth of June with a board of directors and a team of lawyers. If I stand before them single and without any kind of a divorce attached to me, I can defeat the current board president." On the river far below, a log floated by and, mesmerized by it, I watched it bob up and down until it became a speck of brown and disappeared.

"That doesn't make any sense. What does that have to do with me?"

I shut my eyes and inhaled slowly. There was so much I wished I could say to him. "I can't go into details, I'm sorry. I've already said so much more than I ever thought I would."

Theo leaned on the railing and brushed his arm up against me. "So, if I'm hearing you correctly, you're saying you need to be single to take on the board?"

"Precisely."

"What kind of weird stipulation is that?"

If only Grandpa had mentioned something, but it wasn't like he knew he was going to die right away. His health was perfect – just a freak automobile accident. "It was part of my grandfather's will."

"Of this company he owns?"

"Yes."

"And why would you want to be the current board president?"

"Because the guy running it now, should the meeting not go the way I hope, he plans on dismantling it and selling it off. It'll net him hundreds of millions and will take away all the goodness Grandpa worked hard to build. He'll change everything the company stood for." I tried keeping the plea and desperation out of my voice.

"I still don't know how I'm involved in this, and what your being single has to do with any of that."

I tightened my grip on my clutch and avoided looking at him in the eyes. I was words away from showing this wonderful man how truly selfish I was. "You see, the thing is, Grandpa willed his shares in the company over to me, and paired with my own, well, I had majority control over the business and its direction. When I found out we were married, those shares got split."

Theo's face contorted as he processed what I was saying. For the time being, he was a multi-millionaire, he just didn't know exactly how multi. But it wasn't going to happen. I had to yank the rug out from under him, taking it all away.

"And with that division of the shares, I lose control, and the other guy wins. There is a grace period after Grandpa's death to reallocate the shares, and I have until the twenty-sixth to prove I'm single and retain ownership, thus ensuring to continue his legacy."

Theo cleared his throat. "We're not talking about a small potatoes operation, are we?"

I shook my head. *Please don't ask for the company name. Please. I have a different last name for that very reason, so I can make my own way on my own merits, not because I'm the grandchild of Merryweather-Weston.*

“And my part of the shares, because of our marriage,” he air quoted the last word, “would affect your full ownership?” He kicked at a loose pebble on the bridge and picked it up, hurling it over into the river.

“The combined shares, Grandpa’s and mine before they get split, give me controlling shares of the company, and without it…” Mr. Pratt would get his wish. Although selling the company bit by bit would make me richer than my dreams could ever imagine, it wasn’t what I wanted. It wasn’t what Grandpa would’ve wanted either. That kind of money could buy the best research lab and I could branch out of my own, without the assistance of the university. But that wasn’t the dream.

“Can I ask what company?”

“Would I have to tell you?”

He ran his hands through his hair and blew out a long breath. “No, I can respect your privacy on that, I suppose.” He paced a few steps away and spun on his heel. His mouth opened but no words came out.

“I’m sorry,” I said, my shoulders falling inward. “This is bigger than you and me, and maybe after the annulment,” *and a giant cooling off period,* “we can start over. Because I do like you, but I can’t be legally attached to you right now.”

Another couple walking on the bridge stared at us.

The male part of the duo turned to me. "Ouch, lady."

I tried to ignore him and kept my focus on the man in front of me. After a few breaths of wind passed between us, Theo walked back in my direction.

"You're choosing your business over me?"

Yes. I wasn't proud of it, but it was what it was. The kicker of the whole thing was timing… If only we'd met later. "I'm sorry. I said I was going to be honest."

"You were."

It was a lot to take in, and from his viewpoint, probably a lot to give up as well. Not that he was likely hurting for cash, but the shares he was legally entitled to at this moment, they'd be able to put his grandkids through the best universities and then some. He'll never know hardship like my Grandpa had in getting the company off the ground, trying to provide for his family.

He huffed and continued pacing around. It was breaking my heart to see him so stricken, and I hated myself for being so selfish. Finally, after a lifetime, he walked back over to me. "I'm a man of my word. I said I'd grant you the annulment as long as you came with me to the wedding and I'll honour that."

"Thank you." The words fell like a lead weight out of me.

"Can you do me a favour tonight?"

I nodded. Almost anything was within reason.

"Let's go to the wedding and act like there's not this giant cloud hanging over us. Let's go and party, and not give a damn about the outside world. Let's go and enjoy the hell out of a night of fun."

I placed my hand into his. "Sounds like a plan."

# # #

We arrived at the reception a little after five.

"There you are," Natalie, Theo's youngest sister said after running up to us at the entrance of the convention center. She gave me another hug. "Are you going to sit with us?"

"Who is us?" Theo raised an eyebrow, and the smile he gave his sister relaxed his shoulders. Slowly, he was starting to loosen up.

"Amanda and Robbie, Mom and Dad for sure. Come join us."

"Of course," I said to Natalie, and winked at Theo.

Natalie grabbed my hand and wove me through a variety of tables, to one set off to the side. "Sit here."

Mr. Breslin rose as Theo pulled out my chair. "Good to see you again, Izabella." Once I was seated, he sat down. "I'm sorry, it's probably rude of me to ask, but did you take our family name? Or did you stick with your maiden name?"

"No, sir, I stayed with Richardson. It was easier." Given that he knew about the drunken marriage, I would've assumed he understood that I had kept my own name.

"Dad," Theo said with a rumble in his voice. "You promised to not bring it up."

Mrs. Breslin narrowed her gaze at me, but no words breathed out over her rose-coloured lips.

Amanda, sitting beside her mother-in-law, leaned over. "Tell me, how did the two of you meet? Theodore's never shared your meeting with us."

"Well," Theo began, the dimple in his cheek deepening with his grand smile.

I wondered how much he would change or embellish. Instead, as he regaled our meeting to his family, insignificant details I'd forgotten started to surface. "You really remembered the colour of the satin on my dress?"

"How could I forget? It matched the colour of your eyes." A tinge of blush tinted the apples of his cheeks. It wasn't strong like the darkening I'd normally get.

I rested my chin on my palm and gazed upon him with delight and interest. "What else do you remember?"

"Your giggles on the Stratosphere rides. That deep

belly laughter."

That was a fun memory. "You screamed so loud; I'm surprised you remember me laughing."

"I didn't understand why you were laughing. It was maddening, as it was so terrifying especially when it dangled us over the strip."

"That's why I was laughing. I tend to do that when I'm scared." I linked my fingers through his. "That last ride was the worst."

"That, or the ride in the elevator down?"

Oh yeah, that. If memory served me correctly, Theo puked in the corner, mostly from fear I thought. I laughed. "Okay, that was bad, but for a whole other set of reasons."

"Do you remember the Elvis impersonator as we walked along the boulevard?"

"Which one?" There was the alien Elvis, the Elvis as a drag queen and Elvis the dog. More Elvises hung out near the Circus Circus hotel than I'd seen in my whole life.

"The alien one."

"All green face paint? He was atrocious."

"Do you remember what he said?"

I remember bits, but it was all a little fuzzy. The alcohol had still been strong in my system. "Something about living life."

"Yeah. How the best memories in life are the ones filled with laughter and the sweetest people." Theo wore the biggest smile.

I tore my eyes away from him and twisted myself around, not realizing how much I had turned towards my husband. As I straightened out, I took in each of the family member's expressions having forgotten they were even there.

Mr. Breslin gazed lovingly at his wife. "Do you remember when we were their age and how in love we were? Just like them. Like they could take on the world and win." He beamed as he nodded in my direction. "That's love right there."

Amanda tipped her head against her husband, Robert Red Beard, and raised her glass of champagne. "To love."

With the others, I lifted my flute and whispered the toast.

Theo clinked glasses with mine and took a sip without saying a word.

Chapter Fifteen

The lovely bride and her dashing groom encouraged the seated guests to join them on the dance floor.

"You know, we never had a first dance," Theo whispered into my ear.

"You're right, we never did."

He leaned closer, his breath tickling me and sending tingles racing though my body.

"There are lots of things we never did." So many. We didn't have pictures taken, there were no rings. Hell, we didn't even consummate our vows.

"We were about nine sheets to the wind."

"This is truth."

He grabbed me by the hand and led me out the dance floor. It was a slow song, one with a beat I could easily melt into. "Come on, this is our chance." Theo put his arms around my waist, and not sure how I should've responded, I put my hands on his shoulder. "What is this, middle school?" He laughed, but I didn't know what to do with my hands. It seemed too formal to have him hold them, and yet I didn't want to loop them around his neck and give any impression that there was more going on. "Like this." In the sexiest maneuver ever, he ran his hands up my arms and pushed them together. "That's better." He gazed at me with a look I hadn't seen before.

We moved in time to the music, listening to Enrique Iglesias, our bodies getting closer and closer with each beat. Beneath my hands, I felt the tight muscles running across his shoulder blades. I stretched a finger out and touched the side of his face, the whiskers prickling my fingertips and sending out currents of tingles to places that had long ago given up on the idea of ever feeling life again. He tightened his grip on the small of my back and pulled in me, so there was nary a breath of room between us.

Relaxing my grip around his neck, I allowed my thumb to graze his cheek and stroke it. His eyes fluttered closed and a soft sigh rolled free of him. Through the song, I continued to stare up into his masculine face and study his features, the slight curve along the ridge of his nose, the distance between his eyes, the perfect way his brows were shaped. The good doctor was good looking. Inching my hand back around his neck, I gently pulled him down until his lips were upon mine and parted them in heady anticipation.

I kissed him hard, and I kissed him soft, enjoying the sensations rocking through my body.

Warm and breathless, I stopped swaying and rose onto the balls of my feet. Theo lifted me up and swirled me around, his lips never leaving mine. Finally, I tipped my head back and gazed into the face of the man who'd somehow managed to steal my heart. "Wow."

He raised his eyebrows. "Wow? Really?"

"That was the best kiss I've ever had."

"If I had more time, I'd show you what else I'm good at. Maybe that will score in your best evers as well." He led me off the dance floor, and sadly, back over to the table. "More champagne?"

I reached for my glass and lifted it while the sweet scent of bubbly delighted my nose. Very unlike a lady, I pounded back the drink. "Come on, Dr. Breslin. My dance card needs some filling."

"Very well," he said, following my lead back out onto the dance floor.

The fast songs got the crowd on their feet, and after a handful of jumping and hopping and throwing my arms in the air songs, the DJ cut to a much slower pace. I loved swaying with Theo as I caught my breath and melted in his arms. Each slow dance ended with a kiss, and a hope for more. And more I suddenly found myself yearning to give him, but I sensed that wasn't about to happen. There was a smidgen of hesitation and holding back from Theo.

The reception was in full swing by time the midnight lunch rolled out, but I was getting tuckered out. It had been a long time since I'd danced so much and drank so hard. I was nowhere near drunk but had definitely crossed into the tipsy territory. However, it was time for Cinderella to find her way back to reality. The clock was about to strike twelve.

"I think I should get going. I don't want to break up your good time here, so I'll just Uber it home." Then I could sneak out and avoid saying goodnight to all his relatives while I slipped out the door in peace.

"Like hell you will." A giant smile spread across his face. "As my date, I must insist like a proper gentleman on making sure you get safely home."

"An Uber would do that."

"Not on my watch." He leaned against the back of a chair and placed his hands on the table. "Besides, I was ready a while ago, but didn't have the heart to tell you."

I nearly melted from his words. "You're safe to drive though?"

"Haven't had a drink since ten o'clock, and there is no buzz to speak of." That was probably the last time he let go of my hand too. We'd been pretty tight ever since that kiss. "Let's just say goodbye to my parents. I think they're still here."

Exactly what I wanted to avoid. It took some searching out, and quick goodbyes to other guests, but we found Mr. and Mrs. Breslin over by the buffet.

"Are you two heading out?" Mr. Breslin had a slight slur to his words.

"Yes, sir," I answered.

Mr. Breslin set his plate down. "I must say, Izabella, it's been a true delight to have met you in person today. For the time being, you are considered my daughter-in-law, and if there is anything I can help you with, and I do mean anything, please don't hesitate to contact me directly." He retrieved a business card from inside his suit pocket. "Even after things are dissolved between you and my son." Why did he have to look so crushed when he spoke?

It broke my heart and reminded me again of just how selfish I was being. I flipped the card over.

"That's my personal number."

"Thank you, sir. You've no idea what this means."

"Maybe I do." He winked, patting me on the arm

Mrs. Breslin wrapped me in a hug and air kissed my cheeks. “I do hope we get to see you again, maybe for dinner later in the week?”

I wasn’t sure how to respond to that, so I nodded like a bobblehead toy. I’d been honest with Theo how important the annulment was and doubted I would see his parents again. Still, there was no reason to be rude.

“Goodnight. It was a pleasure meeting you both.” My fingers wove tightly through Theo’s gratefully when I felt him tug me away.

“Goodnight, Mom and Dad.” He led me through a mess of tables, avoiding groups of people, and out into the main hall. “They sure can lay on the cheese.”

“I thought it was sweet.” Something I could totally see my Grandparents doing.

“Did you want to walk back to my car, across the river, or did you want me to call an Uber?”

I walked over to the main doors and poked my head outside. The winds had picked up and with it, there was a light scent of ozone in it. “It might rain, but I’ll take the chance. I feel like living dangerously tonight.” It may have been the alcohol talking though.

“Whatever the lady wants.”

We stepped outside into the breeze and I relished the coolness upon my heated cheeks. By time we got to the bridge though, even just a couple of minutes away, I was shivering.

"Here," Theo shrugged out of his jacket and I pushed my arms into the sleeves. The scent of his cologne was still there so I breathed it in.

"Aren't you going to be cold?"

"Not possible. Not after tonight."

We walked to the halfway mark on the bridge and I pulled him to a stop. "Sorry, I need to take my shoes off." My feet were throbbing as I hadn't expected to be on them so much. Maybe I should've worn runners like Theo had suggested, it would've been way more comfortable.

I held my shoes in one hand and sighed as the cool from the concrete seeped into the heated balls of my feet.

"Are you going to walk barefoot back to the car?" He looked down at the bottom of my dress.

I lifted it and wiggled my toes. "It's no biggie. And it feels nice. I'll put my shoes back on at the end of the bridge."

Each step was bittersweet. While the concrete was refreshing, the pressure was too much.

"What are your plans for tomorrow?"

"Aside from resting my aching feet? I have a stack of papers I need to go through to locate some missing information but other than that, not much."

"Cool." He left the word hanging in the air. "What do you think about waking up in the morning with me and having breakfast?" His Adam's apple bobbed while he waited expectantly for an answer.

I grabbed the bait and held my breath, wanting to live a little and take a leap, even though I knew I would be cutting him out of my life soon. However, a girl has needs too. "I can make you breakfast in the morning. I'm not a super cook, but I can make a mean omelet."

His eyes sparkled under the glow of the overhead lights and he rubbed his chin seductively. "I have been known to enjoy a tasty omelet."

"Great." I winced as I stepped on a small pebble.

"You okay?"

"Hazard of walking barefooted."

"Want me to piggyback you?"

The thought made me smile, for more reasons than the idea of me riding him. The last time I had a piggyback ride, I was a teen in middle school, and it had been my grandpa who gave me the ride around the office. Recalling the why was impossible, but I could still hear his giggle as he ran the length of the hallway.

"Is that smile a yes?"

I nodded. "I'd love too, but I'm in a dress."

"Just tuck your dress between your legs when you

jump on." He turned his back to me.

As if it were that easy. I tried jumping and tucking, but I didn't get very high.

"Just jump."

"I am."

He laughed. "You can't jump up that high?"

And it wasn't even that high, I was just a lousy jumper. High jump in school was a horrible experience.

"How about you take a run and then jump?"

That sounded more appealing, and maybe even doable. With visions of Baby from *Dirty Dancing* flying through my head and my shoes gripped between my fingers, I ran a few feet and lunged. Thankfully, he'd lowered himself enough that I actually landed on his back, with a quick readjustment on his part. Definitely not a sexy *Dirty Dancing*-like move.

I held on for dear life, squeezing tightly around the top of his chest.

"I promise, I won't let go."

There was no doubt in my mind of the double meaning of those words.

Chapter Sixteen

It didn't take long for my dress to puddle on the floor and for his tuxedo jacket to drape over the knob of the bedroom door. In a quick movement, Theo had me wrapped in his strong arms while his lips kissed the life out of me. And every breath I breathed in, it was him filling my soul and senses with a tenderness and carnal passion I never knew existed, or knew was the lifeline I was desperate to cling to. It wasn't just hot sex, and it certainly wasn't making love, but a fusion of the two that made me feel both needed and desired, and not just in a sexual way.

"Theo." His name breathed off my lips.

"Izabella." My name became a melody while his hands sweetly caressed my heated skin. Over and over again, until my breath became ragged and sweat beaded all over my body.

It was ecstasy in the best form, pure and natural.

Endorphins raced and flooded through my body, from the ends of my hair entwined in his fingertips, to the tips of my toes curled around his muscular legs. And in the aftermath, our bodies no longer physically connected, we lay wrapped together, our souls beating in rhythm.

Theo fell asleep in a heartbeat, mumbling incoherently as he drifted away. I watched as sleep took him over, seeing the muscles in his cheeks relax at the same time as the strong arm beneath my fingers loosened. Tracing a fingertip over his nose, he twitched, and I held my breath until he stopped. I brushed my fingers through his soft hair.

"Why couldn't you have happened a few months from now?" I whispered into the air. There was an upcoming conference in Seattle in August, and the major one in Vegas in October; meeting him at either of those would've been perfect. Grandpa's company would be safe and secure, and I wouldn't have to worry about Mr. Pratt and his scheming. I'd be free to give my heart away to this wonderful man.

I sighed and rolled out of bed, slipping into a fresh nightshirt. Leaving the slightly snoring man to sleep in my bed, I padded down the hallway and stared at the mountain of sorted piles in my living room. Two new boxes had been added, but those had belonged to my mother. After her passing, her personal files at the office had been boxed and put in storage. Until I'd seen a copy of her Last Will and Testament in the main business portfolios, going through them hadn't been a priority. Now, it seemed urgent.

Folder after folder under the low wattage of a table lamp, I flipped through the stapled papers. There had to be something I'd missed in my random searching. More flipping, and a papercut from not paying attention. However, it wasn't the razor of blood on my index finger that caught my attention. Hidden between two test scores was a letter. Addressed to my mother.

My eyes darted around, not that I was about to get caught doing anything wrong, but it felt like snooping to even be holding the blue envelope. The folder lay flat, the space where the letter had been tucked away for years wide open like a gash. I lifted the flap, pulled out the folded pages and jumped to the last page. I was only going to read it depending on who it was from.

The letter was signed Colby, in a beautiful cursive that suggested more than just a work document.

Instant bubbling rage at the fact that he was connected to my mom swirled through me. How could she not tell me?

I leaned against the back of the chair and crushed the edge of letter into my palms. If it had been from

Grandma, it wouldn't have bothered me, and I would've tucked it back away without a further glance. But it came from him… the man who was out to destroy the family business. Anger pulsed through me, and the emotions of the day combined with the lateness of the night, caused tears to roll out of me. I shuddered imagining Mom and Colby together. She deserved true love, not him. How had he manipulated her into giving him part of her ownership?

"There you are." Theo's sleepy voice broke through the tornado of angry thoughts.

"Hey." I wiped away the tears and tipped my head up.

"What's going on?" His eyes fell to the assortment of papers set around me like a fence.

"I think I'm just over tired."

"Mmhmm." Dressed only in his boxers, he sat down as close to me as he could get without disrupting the piles.

The letter un-crinkled as I relaxed my hand. Theo was an impartial party… "Would you do me a favour?"

He gave his eyes a rub. "Of course." His voice was still gravelly with sleep.

"Can you read this and tell me if it's something I should read?"

Theo reached out to pull the letter away from me.

"You'd need to let go first."

I failed to unlock my fingers and pass it over.

"Maybe it's best if I don't read it. Whatever it is, it's clearly personal." His hand fell to his lap.

"Just read it." I thrust it back at him, and it left my hand without a fight this time.

His brows furrowed, then relaxed, then a small smile played on the edge of his lips. After each page of watching his face, the desire to take it away bloomed inside me. I wanted to know what Colby had written that was worthy of a sly smile, and why he'd written it. Finally, Theo finished up and folded the letter back into its tri-fold originality.

"So? Is it bad?" I stretched out closer to him.

He handed me the answers. "Read it for yourself."

I shook my head. "I can't. It feels intrusive." I closed my eyes and worried about what my mom would think if she knew I was going through her deeply personal and private things. There was a reason she'd hidden this letter between tests. Had they been an item when she was in university?

"Well…" There was a hint of hesitation in his tone, but he pushed through that. "Whoever this guy is, he loved your mom. It's raw and there's a yearning for her to take him back."

Had she dumped him? "When is it dated?"

Theo opened it back up and read out the date. It was written years before her death.

"I was a freshman in high school." I searched out Theo's face for any sign that I could pull more information out of him. "He really loved her?"

"It seems that way."

"Damn."

"Not what you were hoping for, eh?"

How could she love him? He was evil incarnate. Okay, maybe he wasn't that bad, but still. My mom was a saint. He must've had some sob story that she ate up and felt pity for him. There had to be more letters for Theo to read, so he could help me find the answers. I rose out of my spot and rummaged through another box, sifting through folders, hoping to uncover another hidden gift.

"It's late, Izabella. Come back to bed."

"I can't. Not right now." How long had they been together? Had they dated briefly, and she'd cut him loose? Had he done something to hurt her, and that's why he continued to pine after her? Maybe hidden in the letters was the reason she gave her shares to him, and I could prove that they were unwarranted, and he coerced her into it.

He sighed. "Wake me if you need some help."

It was a little after four in the morning when I walked back into my bedroom no further ahead than where I was when Theo left. I fell into bed and snuggled into my pillow.

###

Sleep evaded me fully and I woke up crabby and cranky four hours later. The handsome Theo was still passed out beside me, flat on his back, the sheet barely covering his lower body. Hot damn. He was the total package. And I was the sucker who'd allowed him into my heart.

What was wrong with me? He needed to go, both home and out of my life. Whatever was happening between us wasn't supposed to happen. I needed to face the judge with a clear mind, and a clear conscience. Somewhere in the middle of all this, I'd messed up big time.

Time was up; it was time for Theo to go. But how? How to kick him out without hurting him? Oh, who was I kidding? Whatever I was about to do, it was going to slice like a knife. A dull-edged knife designed to inflict as much pain as possible on both of us.

I pressed my hand onto his chest and shook him. "Wake up." The wall of chest muscles beneath my hand was strong, but it caused me to pause – the steady lub-dub was stronger than that and I felt it in my palm. "Wake up," I said, leaning closer to his ear.

He slowly stretched out and I pulled my hand away.

"Time for you to go home."

"What?" His voice cracked with sleep, and he craned his neck to check out the time.

"I'm sorry, but you have to go."

A quizzical look crossed his face. "For real?"

I nodded and slipped off the bed, picking up his clothes and placing them on the foot of the bed. "I'll give you a couple of minutes to get dressed."

"You're serious?"

"As a heart attack." Which I was going to have soon if he kept looking at me like he was a wounded dog.

Why did I let him in? My grip on reality had slipped yesterday at some point and I allowed myself to entertain the fantasy of a real man, complete with the best end-of-day sex. It didn't matter if Theo was everything a person could hope for, it wasn't the right time. For me, love was something that would have to wait. There were more pressing matters that demanded my attention.

"Was it something I said? Something I did?"

"This is all on me. Trust me." I crossed my arms

over my chest in a weak attempt to hold myself together.

"I don't get it."

"The fairytale is over, Theo. The clock struck twelve. My real life doesn't include love." My voice had an edge to it, something that never happened.

"What fairytale? Izabella, did you ever think that maybe it was destiny that brought us together in October?"

I huffed, loud and clear. "It wasn't destiny, just a ginormous, drunken mistake." I couldn't even bare to make eye contact with him, and instead focused on the painting above my headboard. "I made a reckless decision and I'm trying to fix it."

"We can make this work. We can talk with my dad and fill out whatever forms are necessary to stop this other guy from taking over." He scooted to the end of the bed and grabbed his dress pants, pulling them on in one quick jump. The edges around his eyes softened and his voice fell. "I think I'm falling in love with you. Please tell me we can make this work. There has to be a way."

The metaphorical knife stabbed my heart and twisted.

"I'm sorry, but I'm not in love with you."

"But, last night?" His voice cracked.

"I was just playing pretend and simply fulfilling my end of the deal. I even threw in some bonuses for being so co-operative." *Like the best sex I've ever had, letting you stay in my bed and filling a void in my life.* "I'll see you at the courthouse on Tuesday. Please don't be late."

I locked myself into the attached bathroom and listened for him to leave. Only when the main door clicked shut, did I allow the tears to fall. I was the absolute worst human being to have walked on the earth.

Chapter Seventeen

Sunday, June 21st

I spent the day in bed doing nothing more than lying beside the spot Theo had occupied. His scent was on the pillow, and remembering all the fun we had the night before caused a new set of tears to break their holds and soak my own pillow. My callousness and selfishness had no boundaries. If I was going to be miserable for the rest of my life, I may as well ensure I did maximum damage to those around me. That way, they'll never come back. Even if I wanted him back so bad.

Damn, Theo was everything I'd ever wanted. He was smart, funny, sexy as hell and he had family. Family that had welcomed me in like I'd been there all my life. I didn't think people like that existed. For most of my life, it was just Mom and Grandpa, and the odd friend here and there, until university when I met Tess and Camille, a couple of first years.

Camille had been coming from the education section on campus over to the sciences in search of Tess and got completely lost. Since I was going that way, I led her and we had an easy conversation. She was fun and carefree. When Tess had been found, both offered to take me for a quick coffee, and we'd been friends ever since.

And it was high time to let my friends find out what a complete wreck I was.

# # #

We met up at an eatery with a patio, in the west end of the city, and since I was first, I was seated outside where I watched the birds sing on the tree branches.

"Iza!" That voice could only belong to Camille, her voice was so melodic and filled with spunk. The blonde-haired beauty made good time to the table, with Tess right on her heels. She stopped dead in her tracks as she stared into my face. "You're not okay, are you?"

I shook my head. "Have a seat and I'll tell you all about it."

Tess covered her mouth as she too took me in.

I didn't think I looked that bad. Yeah, my eyes were red and puffy, but it could be blamed on seasonal allergies. And sure, my hair was in a ridiculous top knot -

something I never did. Even my clothes looked sad – a plain old white tee under a long sweater. It was hardly sweater weather, but I'd been feeling so cold all day, it seemed appropriate.

"What's going on?" Tess sat on my left.

Camille sat on my right.

"So much, actually, that I'm not sure where to start. But I have a lot to tell you. Let's order drinks and appies first." I flagged our server down, and we ordered a round of beers and a couple of appetizers.

"I'll just have a Diet Coke or Pepsi," Camille said to the server. She'd been trying so hard to stay away from alcohol. She wasn't an alcoholic, but she had definitely battled a few of those demons.

"So will I," I told the server. There was no way I was going to make things harder on my friend.

"Me too," Tess added.

Once our drinks were set down, two pairs of eyes stared into the depths of my soul.

"Time to spill the beans. I hate seeing you look so despondent."

Despondent; the exact word to sum up how I was feeling. Completely and utterly hopeless.

"Well…" I swallowed a sip of the cool drink, since my throat had suddenly become drier than the desert.

"Things have taken a weird turn since Grandpa's death."

Tess gave me her undivided attention while tucking her dark hair behind her ears. She had a lovely wave in her hair today, it had a nice bounce to it, kind of like she did lately. Ever since her trip to Mexico where she'd found the man of her dreams, by fluke no less, she'd been more upbeat and happier with her life. I was so proud of the changes she'd made and the butterfly she was becoming. She'd had such a shit boyfriend and job prior to that trip.

"We're waiting," Camille said, wrapping her hand around mine. "And we're here to support you, however we can, you know that."

"I do. And I'm sorry I haven't said anything about this until now, but it's only just happened over the last couple of weeks and I'm still trying to sort through it myself."

"Just let it out. Maybe we can help you sort through it all?" Camille threw a glance at Tess, who nodded in agreement.

I inhaled. "Okay. Here's the thing…" I crossed my legs under the table and flipped my gaze back and forth between my friends. "On Tuesday, I'm going before the judge to get…" I took another deep breath. "An annulment."

"An annulment? When did you get married?"

"And why weren't we invited?"

They wore matching shock and hurt expressions.

"Ladies, until ten days ago, I didn't even know myself that I was married." I filled them in on the wedding, the first meeting with the lawyers and my inheritance of shares and how my entire world was flipping all over. "I'm so confused about everything, I don't know whether I'm coming or going."

"So, what's your plan?" Tess loaded up a slice of baguette with a generous helping of bruschetta and pushed the plate in my direction.

"Well, I'm getting the annulment so that all the inherited shares remain in my name, so the current CFO doesn't get control and sell out the business." I picked my piece of bread into fragments. "It's what Grandpa would've wanted. He was nowhere near ready to retire, and if he were still here, I have no doubt he'd be continuing his expansion and doing remarkable things. He said he wanted to do a collaboration with my research, even though the results were years out as he wanted to get into that part of it as well – not just with setting up the stores that offer it. He wouldn't have made those plans if he was thinking about retiring."

"I agree. I didn't know your Grandpa well, but I

could see him as a pretty intense businessman with an extensive list of big plans."

"Thanks, Tess." I ripped up more bread. "And now that dream of his sits on my shoulders."

"But why?"

I turned to face Camille. "Because I'm inheriting his shares. That's what he wanted. If he didn't think I believed in his dream and big plans, he would've left his shares to someone else. Someone who actually understood the business side of things." The learning curve was way too steep a climb for me to ever master. Mom did it, and did so well, as she learned about it and moved up the corporate ladder quickly – or, given who the President was, was probably gifted her right-hand position. However, she excelled at it, and everyone respected her.

"So, you're going to control the company? With nary a hint of knowing what's going on?" Camille always hit you between the eyes with the truth.

"Yep. I may just turn the reins over fully to the CEO and be a sitting board member rather than one who contributes anything. A silent member. Is that what that term meant?" I laughed at my own expense. I was so ill-prepared but as long as it stopped Colby from selling off the company, I had to do it.

"What did success mean to your grandpa?" Tess

asked, reaching for another slice of bread.

"To be the go-to pharmacy."

"Would you say he was successful?"

I narrowed my eyes at her question but answered regardless. "Of course. The MW chain is everywhere."

"It is." She turned to face one of the local stores visible from where we sat. "And your mom, was that her dream? To be the top dog of that?"

I shrugged, not really knowing. It's all I ever remembered her talking about and doing. "I suppose. She dedicated her life to it."

"Right, so that was likely her dream. And when she passed on, then what?"

"Then a new CEO was appointed, and he's been running it well under Grandpa's lead."

"I see where you're going with this, Tess. Smart." Camille tapped her temple.

"I don't." I was so confused.

"What's your dream? Before all this happened, what were you going to do?"

Now I understood where she was going, and I sighed under the weight of the question. "Dreams get put on hold. Dreams change."

"Maybe, but they don't have to." Tess cocked an eyebrow and loaded up another slice of baguette.

"Merryweather-Weston has never been your dream. Never. You went into microbiology, not business."

"So what?"

Camille chimed in and put her hand up in a stop position to Tess. "Okay, let's approach this from a different direction."

I flipped my gaze between the two ladies.

"Who is this guy you're divorcing?"

"Not divorcing, getting an annulment from."

"What's the difference, you're splitting from him?"

"Actually, in business, it's huge. If I divorce him, he's still legally entitled to half my shares and property and matrimonial assets," to use a phrase Mr. Crowe had used. "But if we get the annulment, it's like I was never married, and everything remains mine."

Camille smirked. "Learn something new every day. Regardless," she wrapped her hands around her glass, "what is this guy like? This Theo."

Well, he was perfect. A man who did his own thing. His family were all lawyers, and he broke trend to be the first doctor, but was still super close to them. He was smart and dedicated to his patients, and super sexy. He was the man who filled my dream card. The key word being dream. But it wasn't my reality.

"Wow, do you see that smile?" Camille asked Tess.

"Indeed. I think someone's been bitten by the love bug." Tess glowed; her own bug had repeatedly taken bites out of her.

"Why can't you be with Theo again?" Tess leaned back in her chair.

"Because I'll lose control of the company." We'd been over this.

"And that's the only reason?"

"Pretty much."

"So, you love him?" Camille jumped in with a brutal question.

Was it love? Or was it the idea of love? Did I wish for it so bad that I was willing to see it in any guy who treated me decently? Our moments together flooded my brain, and images of his sweet face took centre stage. He was so easy to be with, and easy to share my personal space with. I was comfortable around him.

"She doesn't need to answer, Cam. You can see it on her face."

I sighed.

"Heading back to my previous thought process," Tess said. "Your grandpa never took another, did he?"

I shook my head. Grandpa had only had eyes for Grandma, and when he spoke of her, it was true love.

"Your mom, did she ever have true love?"

My insides curdled at the thought. Yeah, she had Colby. Apparently. But kept it hidden. "Not that she ever let on. I mean, I don't even know who my father is." That part of her life she never shared with me.

"But you, you have this amazing life, this job you love going to and this sweetheart of a guy. Why would you give that all up for your *grandpa's* dream?"

"Because. That's the way it is."

"But why?" Again, Camille asked. "It's not your dream. You're the last in your family line. Why do you have to give up your dream to continue theirs? They had their shot, and they did it. Do you really think they'd be up there," she looked up to the heavens, "saying please carry on our dream? Make it bigger and better and sacrifice your own goals."

"It's not that easy." Because it wasn't that simple.

"Sure, it is. You just refuse to allow yourself to be happy." Camille took a long sip of her drink. "Excuse me, I need the ladies' room." She walked away.

"I'd apologise for her, but she's right. You should've heard the advice and comments she flung my way in Mexico about Jon. I thought she was blowing smoke up my ass, and yet, here we are."

Yes, here they were. Still separated by thousands

of miles but deeply in love and fighting to make their goal of being together a reality.

But what was it I wanted? Did I want Theo? My whole heart and soul said yes, a thousand times yes. Did I want Grandpa's business to carry on as it was? Yes, he'd worked so hard for that, and deserved his legacy to live on, and if I could help that, then it was my duty to do so. But I couldn't have both. I had to choose.

Chapter Eighteen

Tuesday, June 23rd

The soft handle of my briefcase was as good a place as any to dig my nails into. I paced outside the main doors of Courtroom 612, passing a couple with a child in between them and another couple who were seated as far apart as they could be on the lone bench outside the doors. Taking a few steps into the middle of the corridor, I glanced at the main doors. Still no sign of Theo. We had five minutes until our appointed time before the judge.

The urge to triple check I had all the correct documentation overwhelmed me. More so than the butterflies that swirled in my gut. No matter what my friends thought the family business came first. It didn't matter that I had feelings for Theo, strong feelings even. That was the way things were always done in our family. Even Mom. She had me but still had to go to college and earn her degree to help run Merryweather-Weston. As important as family was, it was second to work, something my friends just didn't understand.

All the documents and signed papers were there. A simple in and out procedure. Hopefully, if Theo showed up, in twenty minutes this would all be over. Another life lesson added to my growing list. Then onto another court meeting on Friday to claim rightful ownership of the company and sign all the necessary papers there. Maybe by the weekend, I'd be able to relax. Or throw up again.

The glass doors pushed open, and Theo breezed on through, holding his own version of a briefcase. The lines were tight around his eyes and his shoulders carried the weight of Atlas.

"Hey," I said, hoping there was no tension between us. Before we'd foolishly gone and fallen in love, we had made an agreement, and I'd lived up to my end of the deal. Although him being here meant he was also living up to his end as well.

"You have the papers?" A curtness to his voice that hadn't been there before. So much for hoping there was civility between us.

I patted the briefcase for good measure.

The courtroom doors banged open and a male stomped out of the courtroom, followed a moment later by a female with another guy. Her smile was a direct contrast to the first guy's glare, and she whispered to her male friend how her luck had finally changed.

A court coordinator stepped out into the foyer. "Richardson? Breslin?" She glanced around.

"We're up." Anxiety peaked at epic levels. Adrenaline coursed through my body and the shakes were building up at a rapid rate. Squeezing and relaxing my free hand helped a bit but not as much as turning and running away would. I could be at the bank of elevators before my name echoed off the walls.

Theo walked ahead and grabbed the handle, pulling open the door for me. "I may be giving up a wife, but I'm not giving up my manners."

My heart stung hearing that, even though he couldn't give up something he never really had. It was only ten days ago we learned we'd been officially married seven months back. With heaviness in my footsteps, I walked into the carpeted courtroom and took my spot standing behind one of two tables.

The judge, an older lady on the verge of retirement, sat on the bench above us. There was more of a look of boredom on her puckered face than one of curiosity, and for a fleeting moment I worried how the proceedings were going to go.

The courtroom deputy swore us in, and Theo and I

took our seats at our respective tables. I sat on the edge, making myself as uncomfortably physically as I was emotionally.

I opened my briefcase and retrieved the copies of the annulment papers and passed them to the deputy, who passed them to the judge.

Please let everything be correct.

If there were any errors, or anything was missed, we were finished and would have to rebook another time. Based on how long people who didn't pull strings got, that could be well into the new year. That wasn't time I had to spare.

I chanced a glance over at Theo, who sat stern-faced staring only in the judge's direction. The suit jacket was unbuttoned and free at his sides. His dark-coloured shirt matched his mood, and I wished there had been another way to make everything work out that was beneficial to us both. What could I say? I was a lousy human being.

Judge Bowden flipped through the papers, and touched the screen in front of her after every couple of pages. "Everything seems in order."

Relief welled up inside of me. Half the battle was complete. The next was the declaration, and I prayed that Theo would stick to the plan.

A bored expression zeroed in on me over the top of her glasses. "According to the document, you wish to have your marriage annulled?"

"Yes, ma'am," Theo said first.

"That's correct." I squeezed my hands together and looked straight through the tension-filled air into her eyes.

"You were both severely intoxicated the morning of October 19th, is that correct?" If her face wore boredom, it was nothing like the tone flowing out of her mouth.

Theo nodded.

"You need to answer, Dr. Breslin." Her voice lacked compassion.

"Yes, ma'am, that's correct. I was severely intoxicated."

The first barrier; we shouldn't have been able to enter into a contract if we were under mental incapacity.

I cleared my throat and swallowed down the lump. "If the Court can see, my name is misspelled on both the marriage license issued at the venue and marriage certificate filed in Nevada Court. Had I been of sound mind, that would've been corrected immediately."

She made a few notes and eyed me firmly. "According to your statement, you and Dr. Breslin have not been in contact since?"

Theo went to speak, but I beat him to it. Honesty

would be best. "That is *mostly* correct, Your Honour. Prior to Friday June 12th, there had been no contact between Dr. Breslin and me. It was at that time when I presented him with the annulment papers you now have."

"I see." She looked over at Theo. "Is that correct?"

"Yes, Your Honour."

Why won't he look at me?

"And why the delay in getting the annulment?" Her monotonous voice was irritating and starting to rub me raw.

I reined in my sigh to stay professional, and to keep emotion out of it. Mr. Crowe had briefly coached me and reminded me that emotions played no part in a courtroom, and would serve no purpose. Keeping my feelings trapped was proving harder than I expected. "It was during a meeting with my grandfather's lawyers on June 11th regarding the transfer of ownership of his shares in his company that it was brought to my attention. Prior to that moment in time, I had not remembered entering into marriage with Dr. Theodore Breslin." My heart pounded and a tinge of a headache formed between my eyes.

"But you remembered after?" She raised an eyebrow.

"It took some hard recalling, and even after that, the finer details are sketchy."

She tapped her screen and scanned over the papers in front of her. "And the consummation of your marriage vows had not happened?"

My heart hit the floor with a thud; we were under oath to tell the truth. "Not at that time." Heat spread upwards at a rapid pace from my chest, over my face and into my hair. From the corner of my eye, Theo twitched. "We had sex for the first time on Saturday night." My focus fell to the papers in front of me. It didn't matter that it was the best sex I'd ever had; it was now my undoing.

May as well pack up my things. It's done. Better call Mr. Pratt and concede defeat and watch Merryweather-Weston crumple into the ground.

The ticking on the wall clock beat louder with each passing second.

"Dr. Breslin, what do you say?"

"Miss Richardson spoke the truth, Your Honour." He put his hands in front of him and clasped them together. One would think he'd been coached too. No doubt he got the better coaching.

"And both parties are in agreeance to dissolve the marriage?"

I held my breath knowing that wasn't what Theo wanted – he'd been quite clear on that – and waited for his answer.

His voice an even calm. “Yes, Your Honour.”

“Miss Richardson? You haven’t answered.” Her piercing glare punctured into my soul, as if she could see the turmoil inside.

I swallowed, the solid lump in the back of my throat refusing to go away. The annulment was what I wanted, wasn’t it? To save the company, it had to happen. So why couldn’t I answer?

“Miss Richardson, I don’t have all day.” Irritation oozed over her words.

My eyes met Theo’s, the answer hanging between us. He was everything I needed, just completely in my life at the wrong time. Everything I learned about him was new and exciting, and I loved the way he was with his family, the way he treated me. Everything about him. But I had to let him go. I had no choice.

“Yes, Your Honour.” The eye contact between us dropped faster than my heart fell into my stomach. Tears built up and blurred my vision. Blinking them away, I sat ramrod straight while she tapped her screen. Emotion belonged to my girlfriends, not in the courtroom.

“Your Honour?” It wasn’t Theo’s voice.

I turned my head and my shock turned to disgust. *Mr. Pratt. How did he even know this was going on at this time?* I had made no mention of the court date to anyone other than my lawyer, Mr. Crowe, and my friends. But even they didn't know the specific time.

"Excuse me, this is a closed courtroom." For once, her voice wasn't directed at me, but the sternness of it echoed off the walls and caused the hairs on my arms to stand up.

The deputy moved in Mr. Pratt's direction.

"If the court doesn't object, I have important documents that need to be seen regarding the marriage between Miss Richardson and Dr. Breslin." He sauntered over to stand between me and Theo, waving a thick letter-sized envelope.

"Are you a lawyer representing either party?" Judge Bowden leaned closer, her eyes narrowing.

"No, ma'am, I am not." He puffed out his chest.

"Are you a lawyer?"

"No, ma'am."

"Then please excuse yourself immediately. You are not a part of these court proceedings." She snapped her neck to the man standing in front of her raised desk. "Deputy, please escort this gentleman outside."

Mr. Pratt tossed the envelope on my table and turned to walk out. "I'm leaving, I'm leaving. But this isn't over, Izabella." He pointed a finger at me before the deputy pushed him out into the foyer.

Why? Why was Mr. Pratt targeting me?

The deputy returned and stood guard at the door.

"Okay, where were we?" Judge Bowden tapped on her screen before lifting the signed papers. "In reviewing the information presented in your declaration." She eyed the document. "Delayed consummation of the vows aside, you both entered into the marriage with mental incapacity. You were both unable to understand the nature of the contract you were entering, and the rights and duties a married person undertakes."

So far, so good. I waited for her to bang her gavel.

"The court hereby grants the order of a Nullity Decree to Miss Izabella Richardson and Dr. Theodore Breslin declaring your marriage as void. Court adjourned."

Void. The outcome I needed. According to the Courts, it would be as if Theo and I had never married, which meant I retained all of Grandpa's shares. I should be thrilled and happy and ready to dance on the table. Instead, I felt lousy and upset and deeply heartbroken.

Theo gathered up his papers and tucked them back into his portfolio, rising slowly.

I closed my briefcase after adding in the mysterious envelope. Whatever was inside, it wasn't good and could wait to be seen.

I exited behind Theo as we walked silently through

the foyer, and down the hall to the glass doors.

Like the gentleman he was, he held the door for me.

The doors closed behind us and Theo made his way to the elevator, shoulders slumped and appearing so much shorter than I knew he was.

Words failed me. *Do I say thank you?* What did you say to the man who was your legal husband a few minutes ago, but was now no longer? I stepped closer as he pushed the down button.

"Theo?"

A gust of air blew of out him and he leaned a hand against the wall. "Don't."

Don't what? My feet dragged me towards him.

"Stop." His face was taut. "It's over, okay? You got everything you wanted."

So why did I feel so awful?

The elevator chimed and the doors slid open. Theo stepped in and braced a hand against the frame.

I shook my head and took a small slide backwards.

The door closed, and Theo disappeared behind the silver wall.

He was gone, and there was only one thing I could do. I pulled a business card out of my purse, and flipping it over and reading off the address, headed in the only direction I was able to go.

Chapter Nineteen

Thursday, June 25th

I slammed the briefcase closed with more gusto than expected. "Sorry."

The older gentleman in the room smiled affectionately at me. "It's okay, Izabella."

"Is this really going to work?" All day long, we'd sat together compiling notes and putting together facts for my big meeting with the board of directors tomorrow.

Mr. Breslin Sr removed his glasses and pinched the bridge of his nose. "I assure you, it will. Your marriage is null and void, so all your grandfather's shares will become yours, fairly and legally. What you choose to do with them is up to you."

I patted my briefcase. We'd just finished drawing up my Last Will and Testament, as well as other documents that allowed me to divide up my shares as I saw fit. It felt morbid to write my final wishes, considering I was in perfect health, but the stake of the company depended on it.

"And the issue of Mr. Pratt showing up at the annulment?"

"That will be addressed as well."

Considering the only person on 'my side' that knew of the court day was Mr. Crowe, it was all highly suspicious that Mr. Pratt showed up. Something wasn't right, and it would be brought up at the meeting tomorrow. The envelope he dropped on me remained unopened.

"Are you nervous?"

I was. The last two nights I'd barely slept. Too many thoughts swirled like a storm in my head. I'd spent a lot of time at the lab in the evenings. Working on my pet project brought welcome distraction from my real life.

I looked into Mr. Breslin's eyes, the deep lines and wrinkles adding character. When I showed up unannounced at his office on Tuesday afternoon, he greeted me like family. And when I unloaded what was going on, he cleared his Thursday schedule to help me prepare. No wonder Theo was such a kind man; he'd learned it from his father.

"Thank you, sir, for everything." I rose and smoothed out my skirt, stretching my neck from side to side. It had been a long, exhausting day.

I extended my hand out.

"Nonsense." Instead, he wrapped me in a bear hug. "I hug family."

The gesture was so sweet, I wanted to cry, even though after Tuesday that ceased to be true.

He stepped back. "Can I invite you over for supper tomorrow? Adaline is making a roast, nothing fancy."

"As appealing as a homecooked meal is, I will have to pass." Since our conversation had switched from work to personal, I'd been dying to ask all day… "Have you talked to Theo?"

"Several times." I'd received more emotion from Mr. Breslin in enquiring about my business options. This answer was flat and lacked so much warmth.

Leave it to me to get too personal, especially about the one I no longer had any claims to. I'd made that painfully clear. I missed the closeness Mr. Breslin and Theo shared. My own mother had been like a best friend.

I looked down to my briefcase and counted the crosshairs that decorated the outside.

"Where I can council you on legal matters, only you can council what's in your heart. You two will need to decide what's best for you both."

"Would he still talk to me?" I just wanted to let him know that it wasn't how I wanted things to turn out, but I had to do what was in the best interest of the company. If it had been another time and place... Every time I picked up the phone, it trembled in my hands and I didn't have the courage to talk to him, always fearing that he would answer or text me back.

Mr. Breslin packed up his spread of papers and laptop and portable office. "I guess I'll see you tomorrow, 9am sharp. You can count on it."

"Thank you, I truly appreciate everything you're doing." I gathered up my things and walked to the main foyer, with my former father-in-law a half step behind me.

Switching to a more serious tone, he said, "Thank you for choosing Breslin Law. We will work hard for you." This time he extended his hand, to which I shook it.

Effective tomorrow morning, right after my declaration and whatever weird swearing in ceremony the company had for new presidents, I'd be announcing the firing of Morgenstein, Greenback and Filarski and the hiring of Breslin Law. My first executive order. After that shock rippled through the board, I'd unveil my other plans.

Two things were a given. One – I was bound to be well-hated by the board. And two – I wanted desperately to talk to Theo, to hear the reassurance in his voice and to feel him hold me tight and tell me I've got this.

It was too much to feel like I was falling apart.

Chapter Twenty

Friday, June 26th

I strode into the Merryweather-Weston's head office at 8:30am, and greeted the receptionist, who informed me that the big boardroom in the corner was set up and ready for me. The one with the impressive view of downtown from which I could almost make out my apartment building from the south side of the window.

Putting my paperwork in order, I tidied up the end of the table I planned on occupying, saving a seat for my lawyer. The phone buzzed in the boardroom and I pushed the answer button.

"Yes?"

"Miss Richardson, Mr. Breslin is here for you."

For a heartbeat, I jumped and entertained the thought that it was Theo who'd arrived, but then logic took over and reminded me it was his father. "Thank you. I'll be right there." Inhaling sharply, I counted to three and stared at the old picture hanging on the wall by the door – my grandfather standing beside his first store on Jasper Avenue, the flagship store still in business. "Your dream is still alive, Grandpa." I touched the picture for luck and headed to the front desk to meet Mr. Breslin. "Good morning."

After greeting Mr. Breslin, we walked the length of the hall, passing more pictures of Grandpa's startups, including his tenth store where Grandma and Mom and baby me were pictured.

"Set up over there." I pointed to the corner as I closed the door. "Please let me know if there's anything you need. Mr. Breslin."

"You can address me as William, or Bill."

Maybe outside the office, but most definitely inside, he would remain Mr. Breslin. I was too old school to address an elder with anything less than respect.

He set his briefcase on the sideboard behind him and walked over to where I stood. "Are you ready?"

I put my hands out in front of me; they shook like a leaf on a windy day. "No. But I know I will be." Sleep evaded me last night as well, so I was running on about two hours of shut-eye. I tried to have a cup of coffee, but my stomach was in so many knots, it sat like a lead paper weight. I hoped this all went well, but I expected there to be many hiccups and mini battles.

"You'll be fine." He patted my shoulder.

It didn't feel that way, but I was going to go with it. All the dominoes were set up, it was just a matter of knocking that first one down.

###

I was buzzed a few minutes before nine; the receptionist informed me how Mr. Crowe and crew had arrived. Tina escorted them into the room and judging by the shocked look on their faces, they weren't expecting me to have brought back-up.

I sat at the head of the table, with Mr. Crowe on one side of me, and Mr. Breslin on the other. Around the edges of the table wrapped Mr. Pratt and the eleven other members of the board. All focused on me. It was daunting.

"Alright, let's bring the meeting to order." Mr. Crowe shuffled through some papers. "In establishing the presidency of Merryweather-Weston, it is hereby stated that Miss Richardson's shares, combined with the inherited shares from Lloyd Merryweather, make her the president." He glanced around the room.

Mr. Pratt cleared his throat. "Did the annulment get approved?"

I swallowed, afraid to see the disappointment in Mr. Breslin's face. "Yes, it did. The judge granted us the Nullity Decree as we were not of sound mind when we wed in Las Vegas, back in October."

Mr. Pratt's face fell, and a week ago, I would've fought hard to rein in a smug feeling. Instead I felt how he appeared – dejected, sullen, and generally miserable. I missed Theo, his voice and his laugh.

Mr. Breslin produced a copy of the decree and passed it to Mr. Crowe, who then passed it around to the board members. All except Mr. Pratt nodded.

"It's stated, for the record, that Miss Richardson is now the president of Merryweather-Weston." Mr. Crowe scrawled his pen across some notes. "If you'll just sign here." He passed me the paper, and I glanced at it quickly before sending it to my personal lawyer.

Mr. Breslin picked it up, scanned through it and passed it back to me. "It's all good, everything's standard." He tapped the space where I needed to sign.

I picked up the pen and held it over the line, the pen teetering between my fingers. This was it; the start of a new beginning.

The room held its collective breath, and the air went stale. I reached for the glass of water I'd poured earlier.

"Everything okay?" Mr. Breslin whispered under his breath.

I swiped my palm over my forehead and let out a short breath. "It's just such a big moment. A huge deal. I just need to collect my thoughts." Unsure why, I cast my gaze around at the board members and legal counsel staring at me. The longer I delayed, no doubt the more their faith in my position to run this company deteriorated. I held the pen above the line and in the next heartbeat, scratched my signature over it. The only person who let out a breath was me. Just like that, I was now the President of a company I didn't have the heart to run.

I slid the paper over to Mr. Crowe, who opened a folder and slid it inside.

"Now, let's go over a few minor points of your new position, just so all of us are on the same page." Mr. Crowe grabbed a stapled pack of papers from another folder and began.

Across the table, Colby Pratt glared at me, knowing his future plans for this company were as null and void as my marriage.

My marriage.

For a brief time, I was happy. Truly happy. Unexpectedly happy. True love had found me, and I'd cast it aside like a piece of garbage. All in the name of business.

I wasn't shrewd like my mother, and I wasn't savvy like my grandfather. I was weak in terms of the business world – my expertise lay elsewhere. And I wasn't the only one who knew that. My shoulders sagged forward under the weight of my new expectations.

"Stop." The word fell out of me with such power, I was once again the intense point of focus. "Before we go any further, I need to clarify a few things."

"Miss Richardson, we were doing just that." Mr. Crowe pushed his glasses back up his nose. "We're nearly done."

"Fine."

He carried on and I zoned out, which was terrible, but I was trying to work out the next steps in my plan – to have Mr. Pratt admit what he was planning and for someone to account for how and why he'd showed up unannounced at the annulment. Yesterday I had this all planned out, but I couldn't remember the order of questioning I had.

Mr. Breslin tapped my arm.

"What?"

"Miss Richardson," Mr. Crowe began in the most patronizing tone.

"Just wait, I'm thinking."

Someone around the table sighed, and it wasn't me.

"I have a few things I want to say."

Mr. Breslin and I had gone over this yesterday, and thankfully he'd passed me the legal pad in which he'd scribbled down my random notes. Underneath it all was the order he thought it best I ask the questions in. While re-reading it over again, I realized it didn't really matter. I turned my gaze to Mr. Pratt, about to query item six, instead of the topic at the top, which Mr. Breslin had circled for good measure. "I need clarification now on a couple of important matters. Firstly, Members of the Board, I would really like to know what your plans for the company were, if you'd had majority. What direction would you have taken the company in? Oh, and please tell me your name and how long you've been with the company."

One by one, the stunned members gave answers akin to a Miss America contest – they were all basically the same – keep the company moving in the direction Mr. Merryweather had started. Fair enough. I moved through the board members, jotting down their names as they introduced themselves.

The one person I was most interested in answered last. "What about you, Mr. Pratt? What would you do if you had majority? And be honest, I want to move ahead collectively as a group and welcome new ideas."

"Umm…" He wiggled in his seat. "I'd like to try to expand beyond the borders and get footing in the US."

"Interesting."

The members whispered to themselves.

"And you'd like to expand, not reduce?"

"That's correct."

Mr. Breslin tapped a line on the legal pad.

"That's not what Smith Quinn Divestitures Group informed me when I reached out to them on your behalf."

Colour washed out of him and for a heartbeat, I feared he'd lose his breakfast all over the table. Murmurs swirled around us.

I sighed and leaned on the table. "All I want is the truth. Please."

His Adam's Apple bobbed, and he cleared his throat. "The truth."

"Please."

"Okay. We were approached not long after Lloyd's passing about a US based company who was interested in us, but not about expanding. They want to buy us out and bring our brand into the US."

"This is huge," said board member Paul, who'd been with the company for eighteen years. "As the next senior member of the board, this should've been discussed with me, if not all of us."

I scribbled on my legal pad – *what are his shares?* – and passed the paper to Mr. Breslin.

He riffled through his papers and set the sheet beside me. Paul had a modest 10.4%, well below Colby's shares.

"Let's discuss it now, shall we?" I pushed my stomach into the edge of the table. "I don't want there to be hidden agendas and secrets. If we're all wanting the best for the legacy of this company, there needs to be transparency." My own words surprised me.

Colby cleared his throat and divulged the payouts we'd receive and the approximate timeline; all of it. He even explained it in a way that helped me understand for the most part how everything was involved.

Truth be told, it sounded feasible, and would put to rest all my fears. It was well thought out, as if it had been something discussed over months, not weeks. I could sell out and be cleared to go and live my dreams, with more bank than I ever dreamed. All the shareholders would never have money issues.

I quickly looked over at Mr. Breslin. There was no emotion emitting from him, but his hand was scribbling fast across his legal pad. Before I knew it, he had written two full sheets of paper with notes about the possible buyout.

Mr. Pratt stopped talking and pushed back slightly from the table, looking directly at me, slightly flustered, and yet at the same time almost relieved.

"Can I think about it?"

"What?" His jaw dropped.

"I think as a board we all need to sit down and hear what Smith Quinn has to say, and if we're all on board, then we can proceed as a group. But it must be a group decision, no dictatorships here."

"That's umm… really unexpected of you, Miss Richardson."

"You and I both know I'm not a businessperson. My field of expertise belongs in the lab producing the vaccines and pharmaceuticals my grandfather sold."

Mr. Breslin placed his hand upon my arm as if to warn me to stop talking.

I looked around the table at the thirteen men and one woman looking at me. "Would it be okay if Mr. Pratt and I took a few minutes in private to talk?"

"What's this about, Miss Richardson?" Mr. Crowe's head snapped up.

"Nothing business related. It's personal, and I'm not sure if he'd want to discuss this out in the open." I held his curious gaze, tightly. "We'll go to Lloyd's office. Take fifteen and grab yourself a coffee and a snack." I pointed to the spread at the far end of the room. I rose, patting Mr. Breslin's hand. "I'll be right back."

"You're sure you want to do this?"

"Yes."

Mr. Pratt held the door for me, and we walked in silence down the hall to my grandfather's office. After unlocking it, we entered and I sat in Grandpa's chair, directing Mr. Pratt to the chair in front.

"What's on your mind?"

"My mother."

Two words that widened his eyes and softened his hardened expression. "Nora Weston was an amazing CEO."

I leaned back in my chair, crossing my legs. "I know, but I'm not interested in that. I can ask the board and the staff if I want any answers about that. I want the stuff only you can answer."

"And what would that be?"

"Did you have a secret relationship with her? I found a couple of letters she'd kept." I straightened myself up and scooched my chair in, leaning my forearms on the solid oak desk.

He sighed. "It's complicated."

"Love always is."

"She was a beautiful woman and a powerful

business lady, and yes, we had a secret relationship."

"For how long?"

"Twenty years? I loved her from the moment she became staff. A fresh thing out of college, a brain full of imaginative ideas, and as she climbed up the corporate ladder, there was just something between us that clicked. But your grandfather hated the idea of business mixing with pleasure and kept separating us, moving me to a different division, so we kept things quiet. I'd come over when you were in bed, and sometimes, if we were lucky, we'd rendezvous across the country, away from Lloyd's prying. We were secretly happy." There was a twinkle in his eye I'd never seen. "Have you ever been in love, Miss Richardson?"

Yes, and I just got an annulment from him. I shrugged, never giving him an answer. I wasn't here to discuss my life, just his involvement with my mother. "What about her will? I noticed it was changed after her illness."

"Funny you should ask about that." He chuckled and clasped his hands behind his head. "Your mom wanted to sell her shares to an outsider before she died, but I talked her out of that. Nothing malicious, just trying to keep the shares close. Then she wanted to give them all to you even though at that point you were fresh out of college and not at all interested in the family business. She wanted you financially protected. But she decided against that at the last minute – didn't want to burden you with the stress of something like that."

That was news to me, but good news. Mom had understood that going into the family business wasn't a dream of mine. I leaned in closer to listen, and hear everything Mr. Pratt was saying.

"The shares she wanted you to have, they were transferred to me, and are earmarked to be given back to you. Should anything have happened to me, you would've been willed those shares."

I lifted my jaw up off the desk.

"I can tell you never read what was in that envelope."

The one he showed up with at my annulment. I shook my head.

"Mr. Filewick has all the details on that, and inside that envelope was the letter she signed stating how I had her shares, and how I could transfer them to you at any time. Even with your half from your grandfather, your other earmarked shares would've given you majority."

That was huge, and those shares amounted to quite a bit. "And you knew this that day a couple of weeks ago?"

"When your grandpa died, the board knew you

were getting all of Lloyd Merryweather's shares. You had majority, no contest. But when the marriage certificate showed up, those were cut in half."

"Right, but those earmarked shares could've pushed me over. I wouldn't have had to get the annulment." I could have had the best of both worlds, instead of being forced to choose.

"Like it or not, you needed the annulment. The company needed it. No one knows anything about this guy. It was in the best interest of everyone involved."

"Who's *everyone*?"

"The shareholder board and the board of directors."

They all knew. My mouth dried out and I was suddenly wishing for a glass of water.

He pulled his chair closer. "I'm sure you think of me as the enemy, and why wouldn't you? I haven't given you a reason to see me as anything but, so let me assure you, I have nothing but your best interests at heart. That and Nora's." He looked toward the ceiling. "I really loved her. I had a change of heart and went against the board's decision. You were supposed to read what was inside that envelope immediately and end the annulment proceedings."

"But that would have left those shares with Theo."

"It was worth the chance. I did some research on

him, and he's a good guy, Miss Richardson. And his family name is a good one too. Your mom would've been proud of him."

A dull ache formed in my heart. "Did she love you?"

"With all her heart."

"Why didn't you go public with it?"

He shrugged and tugged on his sleeve. "Lloyd, mostly. There were several other reasons too, but they're not up for discussion."

Fair enough. He'd already told me more than I'd ever expected to hear.

"Nora wanted you to live your best life, in whatever way that was meant to be."

"I don't know what that is yet."

"Yeah, you do. You just need to look in your heart. Start fresh. Live hard. Love harder." He put both feet on the floor. "Is there anything else you wanted to ask me?"

Nothing came to mind.

"Take a few minutes and come back to the boardroom." He rose and walked over to me, putting his hand on my shoulder. "You've got this, President, and we'll make your dreams come true."

The door closed with a click and I took in the surroundings. All of Grandpa's framed photographs and his lifetime of achievements decorated the space. That had been his dream, and he'd fulfilled it better than anyone I knew. He'd worked hard and made the choices. He'd lived his dream.

And now, it was time to live mine.

Chapter Twenty One

I held my head high when I walked back into that boardroom. I felt older, more mature and surprisingly, the world didn't seem as angry as it had been just an hour ago.

The chatter in the room died as I opened the door.

"Thank you for that break." My eyes scanned the room and stared at the clock. I'd been gone much longer than the short fifteen minutes I said I'd take. "I apologize for the delay. If you'll just finish getting some snacks, we'll pick up where we left off." I took my place beside Mr. Breslin.

"Everything okay?"

A smile formed on the edge of my lips. "Never better."

The shareholders and legal counsel sat down, and we got under way.

I folded my hands together and inhaled softly,

breathing out the stress I'd been hanging on to. "In light of the possible selling off of Merryweather-Weston, I would like us to schedule a full meeting with Mr. Pratt's contact at Smith Quinn. I'd like all board members present as well as the board of directors. I'd also like Legal there to make sure everything is on the up and up. I want to hear what our options are. I'd also like to know how you all truly feel about the possibility of being bought out?" There was no way, as the last possible President of the company, I would allow the staff to suffer. If this was going to happen, everyone was going to come out on the winning side. "Mr. Pratt? Can I leave you in charge to schedule that please?"

"Of course, Miss Richardson."

"Thank you." I ran over the checklist Mr. Breslin had pulled out for me. None of it seemed relevant now. The one thought process I had with regards to Mr. Pratt had been let lose, derailed everything.

He tapped his pen beside a couple of points.

"I won't bother." They were minor and inconsequential in the grand scheme of things. I addressed Mr. Crowe. "Is there anything else we need to go over?"

"No, Miss."

I made eye contact with every person around the table. "Does anyone have anything they want to bring up? Anything I've missed?" No one moved. "Nothing?" Had my grandfather been so strict that they were afraid to answer? "I guess we're done and will be back together as soon as Mr. Pratt informs us of the next meeting."

One by one, the room cleared out, with Mr. Pratt being the last.

When the room belonged only to me and Mr. Breslin, I sunk into my seat with an exhausted sigh. The adrenaline surges I'd been privately dealing with were done and my legs were as weak as wet spaghetti.

"Well done." Mr. Breslin packed up his things. "You walked in here and owned the room. You should be proud."

It was almost noon. The meeting had gone on longer than I'd expected, I'd planned for a full day of boardroom time and now had time to kill. As much as I wanted to go to the lab, even though I'd taken the day off, it was best for me to hang around the office. Read up on the hiring process. Maybe. Just in case the whole Smith Quinn purchase was a joke, I should consider hiring someone for my president role, since I really still didn't know what I was doing. I'd be a pretty weak president if I kept deferring ideas to someone else.

"You know, dinner still stands for tonight?"

"Wouldn't that be a conflict of interest?" I laughed, but only because if I was still married to Theo, then it could be a conflict of interest having the father-in-law run Grandpa's business, er, my business.

"Only professionally if you were still interested in my son, but since you are no longer together, it's not a problem."

"But what if I was?"

He cocked a silver eyebrow. "Still interested in my son?"

I nodded.

"Then you'd want to make sure you come for dinner." He winked and passed me a legal-sized sheet of paper. "My address. Supper's served at seven."

Chapter Twenty Two

I finally accepted an invitation to supper at the Breslin residence, after Mr. Breslin contacted me a month after my becoming President. Despite my hesitation, he assured me it wasn't against a code of ethics as it would be no different than having a client over, something he and the missus did regularly. It had taken a considerable amount of effort for me to say yes because, despite his saying so, he wasn't family, even if that's what I wanted.

However, a month after I accepted the presidency, I turned the radio to low while I circled the neighbourhood looking for the Breslin residence. Before I'd left my apartment, I had a rough idea of where I was going, but now that I was in the schwanky area, I was lost. These houses were huge. I pulled out my phone and opened Google maps. Slowly, I inched my car down the winding road and turned on to the right street.

The Breslin house was a much smaller bungalow than I expected, based on the size of the two-story manors with four-car garages I passed on the street. I drove my car into the wrap around driveway and cut the engine. From the backseat, I pulled out a $40 bottle of wine, the least I could bring to supper, as well as a potted orchid. Suddenly, I was more nervous at entering their home than I was in the board meeting a few weeks back, and I'd been on the edge of hysteria then.

Breathing deeply in a weak effort to calm myself, I walked up the stone sidewalk and rang the doorbell.

Mrs. Breslin opened the door. "Good evening, Izabella. I'm so thrilled you decided to join us. Please, won't you come in?"

I stepped into a massive foyer – my kitchen and dining area took up less space – and glanced around. The place oozed wealth, with a classy designer's touch of greys, blacks and a pop of green. Instead of a cold, institutional feel, it was warm and inviting. It reminded me of Grandpa and Grandma's home back in the day, except theirs was smaller.

"This is for you," I handed her the plant, "and the wine's for dinner."

"Thank you." She air-kissed my cheeks before freeing my arm of the weight. "Come on back."

"Did I hear the doorbell ring?" Mr. Breslin rounded the corner. Gone was the standard issue suit I'd always seen him in, replaced with a more casual look of shorts and a sweater, but he seemed more relaxed in his attire than Mrs. Breslin did in her pant suit. "Well, if it isn't Izabella." His voice boomed off the walls, and he wrapped me in his fatherly hug. "So glad you finally decided to join us. You'll see, we don't bite." He laughed as he led me to the back of the house, into the kitchen.

I was glad to be here as being with the Breslins gave me something I'd missed out on – family. Not that I didn't once have a family, but Mom had always been working and Grandpa too. We didn't do the dinners around the table; we ate together in boardrooms or around desks. But that had been years ago…

Being in the Breslin's kitchen was like something out of a dream. The kind you didn't want to wake from. There was easy chatter between Mr. and Mrs., and soft jazzy music played. The space was bright and airy, but it was the smells that did me in. Whatever she was cooking, it was tantalizing to the taste buds.

"What can I help with?" It was too formal to call her as Mrs. Breslin, and yet, I wasn't comfortable enough to call her Adaline, so I didn't address her at all, but stood close enough so she knew.

"Never you mind; you're a guest. Pour yourself a glass of wine and head out onto the deck. I'll be a minute or two behind you." She handed me a crystal wine glass and Mr. Breslin filled it from the already open bottle of Merlot.

"Just through the screen doors." He pointed over to the edge of the kitchen. "I'll be right out."

A beautiful deck sprawled across the length of the house, and an oversized red umbrella covered one end. Beyond that was a small forest of greenery with a clearing that led to the most amazing view of downtown.

"Wow." My voice came out a whisper.

The screen door slid open and Mr. Breslin breezed out. "Have a seat."

I sat in a comfy, oversized patio chair. Even better, it had a gentle rocking motion and I pushed myself into a leisurely rhythm.

Mr. Breslin laughed. "That's Theodore's favourite too."

I scanned the area. There wasn't an abundance of seating options so it's not like he had a lot of choices. I dismissed the comment with a wave and tipped my head down. "He won't return my calls."

"Give him time." He set his wine glass down on the low table between my chair and the one he'd decided to occupy. “He opened his heart–”

“I know.” And I crushed it. “I’ve tried to call and apologize, but…” Not that I’d blamed him.

“Did he ever tell you about his former girlfriend?”

I shook my head. His friend Garrett had mentioned something, but Theo shut it down quickly.

“I won’t go into details, but she did a ringer on him. It was so bad we all worried he’d never bounce back. But he did, after that trip to Vegas, even if neither of you truly remember getting married,” he winked as if I’d been holding back some sort of truth all this time. “Theo became full of life again. Maybe it was your rollercoaster thrills, I’ll never know, but frankly, I’d like to think a huge part of his turning around was you. You brought him out of his funk and gave him hope.”

And now I had guilt. It wasn’t enough that I felt horrible for lying to him, to get him to leave because I was falling for him, now I had guilt that my actions may have caused him to regress. I swallowed a few too many sips of the red wine as Mr. Breslin waxed on about his son.

“You probably already know this, but Theo doesn’t do anything half-assed. It’s all or nothing with that boy, and always has been.” He drifted away in a haze. “Ever since he was a kid, once he set his mind to something, whether it was his academia or his sports, he pursued it, even if he didn't like it. He had to prove he wasn't going to fail at it." He shook his head and drank some of his wine. "Anyways, now he's operating his own evening clinic twice a week, in addition to the hours he puts in at his day job, as he calls it. He's back to being a workaholic. And that's not healthy."

I knew he was a dedicated doctor, but I hadn't known about his own private clinic.

"Same as you – you both give work your all."

That I couldn't argue. And lately, that was all I did. I had flipped my lab hours to afternoons and evenings so I could spend the mornings being immersed in all things Merryweather-Weston. By time I got home at nine or ten o'clock at night, I was worn out. There was no way I was going to be able to maintain this pace for much longer. Just a few more months…

"Speaking of work, what did you decide?"

Ah, yes, the buyout. "We've agreed to it all, it was pretty much a unanimous decision. As of the new year, Merryweather-Weston will be operating under a new name, new board and mostly new management team. We need to finish out the fiscal year as we have two major conventions planned." One in Seattle next month, and the mother of all conventions in October in Vegas. "Plus Mr. Pratt and I are flying all the franchise owners in for a meeting in the fall to go over the terms of the new ownership."

"That's a big undertaking."

I tucked my legs underneath me. "It's what Grandpa would have done. He wouldn't have left his franchisee owners hanging, or pulled the rug out from under anyone, and I intend on trying my best to stay true to his vision. For as long as I can."

"And you're okay with the sell out?"

"It sounds so terrible, right? Like I've given up? But I need to do what's best for now, with what I'm capable of." My finger absently ran along the edge of the wine glass. "Lloyd Merryweather and his daughter, Nora Weston, had their dream and succeeded beyond their wildest dreams. It's my turn."

"You need to do what's best for you."

"Thanks."

Many nights when I couldn't sleep, I'd talk to my Grandpa and to my mom. The night before our meeting with Smith Quinn a peace I'd never felt before blanketed me, and in my heart, I was confident that I was making the best decision. Everyone at Merryweather-Weston was going to be very well taken care of, either in a huge buyout with their shares or lucrative settlements. Some, at least for now, will continue their roles, just under the new banner.

With my payout, starting in January, I'd be working under my own company name – a research company dedicated to cancer prevention, not to finding the cure, but to find the way to stop the cells from activating in the first place.

The figurative light went on late one night and until the sun came up, I scribbled out the new direction to take my research in. And who knows, maybe I'll find the preventive medicine – if you will, that will stop any cancer, or more importantly, pancreatic cancer. Maybe the company taking over Grandpa's will be able to fulfill that dream of distributing it. Time will tell.

"You came?" The delighted squeal from Theo's little sister echoed through the open patio door as she came bursting out onto the deck. "I'm so happy to see you again." She dropped down into a lounge chair. "Is Theo coming too?" Natalie looked right at her dad as she asked.

"Not tonight, honey."

"Darn." The teenager jumped her gaze from me to his father and back again. "You're going to get back together, right?"

"Natalie Breslin, you know better than to ask that."

I whipped my head around, surprised to hear Mrs. Breslin's voice bolt from the window.

"Sorry, Mom. Sorry, Izabella."

I took another sip of my wine.

"When's dinner so I can go call him. I need his help with some biology homework." She tucked her chin in and her light brown hair fell beside her cheeks.

"You're in school?" It's July.

"Summer school."

"And it's biology homework you need help with? May I? I loved bio in high school."

"That's right, you're a scientist." Her eyes went large as they lit up. "I'd love your help." She jumped out of her chair and ran back inside, only to return a moment later with a heavy textbook and binder.

"What are you studying?"

"Genetics and DNA." She pouted. "It's so hard."

"You should come to my lab and see it all in real time. It might change your mind on it."

"Are you serious? I'd looove that." Her smile was a dead ringer for her brother's.

I glanced over to Mr. Breslin, a small smile crossing my own face.

He gave me a wink. "I'll leave you two ladies to chat while I go help Adaline." He rose with a huff from his seat and reached for my wine glass. "I'll also top this up for you."

Four hours later, my tummy sore from laughing and my heart full from the gathering, it was time for me to go.

"Thank you for inviting me over." I rose from the patio chair.

Natalie followed closely on my heels. "Thanks again for the biology help."

"Anytime. Give me a call on Monday and you can come by the lab."

"I'd like that." With that she reached out and wrapped her arms around me.

Normally, I'd bristle at the contact, but I found myself hugging her back even tighter. And enjoying it.

"Thanks again for supper and the dessert." It had been the best way to spend a Friday evening in a long time. I grabbed my purse and headed to the front door.

Mrs. and Mr. Breslin followed me to the foyer.

"Don't be a stranger. You're always welcome here." Mrs. Breslin opened the door.

Lights flashed across the front of the house from a car pulling onto the driveway.

"Who could that be?" she asked her husband.

Mr. Breslin cleared his throat. "Theodore. He texted about an hour ago that he was coming over."

I didn't want to see the expression on Mr. Breslin's

face, for fear I'd overstayed my welcome. With a quick wave goodbye, I made my way down the stairs, hearing my heart thrum in my ears. I rounded the corner and nearly bumped into the good doctor. "Hey," I breathed out. It had been a long time since I'd seen him and, truth be told, even though he looked worn out and ragged, he was still charming and handsome.

"What are you doing here?" He cast his gaze to the front porch where the screen door closed, and back to me.

"I was just leaving."

"Theo," Natalie said, suddenly emerging through the door. Saved by the sister.

"Were you here on business or pleasure?" His eyes met mine.

Natalie answered before I could even let a breath out. "She came for dinner, and on Monday, she's going to take me to her lab, and I can see things through the microscope."

"Nat, can you excuse us please?" He didn't even look at her.

I did, and her face fell straight onto the ground.

"I'll be inside in a minute."

"But I…"

The low throat clearing sound that came out of him must've been a big brother type of warning. Her shoulders rolled in and she turned away. "G'nite, Izabella. See you Monday."

I waved at her back.

"Let's get something straight," Theo said, a tinge of edginess on the tip of his tongue. "This is my family. I may be the black sheep of it, but they're mine. You can't weasel your way back to me through my parents or my sister. Do you have any idea how sick and twisted that is, to use her to get to me?"

Being stabbed with a rusty fork would've caused me less pain. I definitely wasn't doing any of that. "That's hardly fair. Your dad invited me for supper." I was sensible enough to get to him through him; by phone, text and even a feeble attempt at a fax to his office but Theo had ignored every attempt I'd made.

"Just stop, okay? You made it pretty clear that you and I were a huge mistake. It's been erased from the courts and your personal records, and you've moved on. Time to let me move on as well."

I hardly thought I'd moved on. My every second thought revolved around him, or a memory of him.

"They're not your family."

"I know that." A slow fight was building in me. The glowing embers of anger fanned into flames. "Listen, I'm allowed to visit with whoever asks me."

"Not them."

"Why not? It was no different than meeting with a business associate." Until Natalie came home, and Mrs. Breslin made the most mouth-watering meal I'd ever eaten. Until the gentle snickers turned into full body laughs over something as silly as a movie we all adored. It was during that laughter, I'd felt the switch. From business to pleasure. Yeah, I guessed that was why.

"Find your own family. Leave mine alone." Theo stormed away, only to spin on his heels and march back. "Why in hell would you hire Breslin Law to represent your company?"

I stepped back and shook my head while narrowing my eyes. "Not that it's any business of yours, but I didn't hire them for the company; I hired your father as my personal lawyer. He helped me write my will and settle a few personal things with regards to my grandfather's estate." Suddenly, like I'd been punched in the gut, my fight was gone. I had no desire to relive any of that. I shuffled toward my car and clicked it unlocked. My hand was on the door when Theo appeared beside me.

"Tell me something," his voice was low. "Was the sacrifice worth it?"

It was a double-edged sword, that's for sure. I gained the company, but with it came the loss of the one thing left in my life that mattered most to me. Theo. I loved him, but…

"You don't have to answer. I completely understand family dynamics."

As the only doctor in a family of lawyers, I was sure he'd dealt with more than I would know about or understand. "Would you have done the same thing?"

He sighed. "I don't know. Maybe. Maybe not." He stepped back, putting some distance between us. "But I would've found a way to make it work. I like to work in the grey. You clearly are black or white."

"And I tried." There was no other way. I'd searched, and I'd spoken with a lawyer about it.

"Not hard enough." The distance between us grew, the cold hard truth cutting a giant gash from his heart to mine.

"But I've tried to get in touch with you. You've refused all my calls, and my texts go unanswered." The tears wouldn't stop but for once, I didn't care. "Please don't leave."

"Then you'll know how it feels to lose someone important."

I wiped my hands across my face, pulsating insta-rage coursing through my body. "I know more about losing the most important people in a person's life than you ever will." My anger lashed out with my words and I yanked open my car door. "Don't you get it? I'm an orphan. I have nobody!" My fingers dug into the metal of the door. "You don't have to worry about my calls ever again. Now I'm through with you."

"Good. Go and find a new family. Go break someone else's heart. There's nothing left for you here anymore."

I started up the car and drove as far as I could until I couldn't see anymore and pulled over on the side of the road. Tears fell and my heart hurt so much, I thought I was having a heart attack.

Chapter Twenty-Three

August

I glanced out into the audience, finishing up the last of my speech. It had been a whirlwind three days of lectures and speakers, and I for one was glad it was over. I'd learned so much and was excited to get back home and work in the lab, since there was no point in getting the company on board. The papers had been signed. Merryweather-Weston was closing shop on December 31. Now, my energies could be focused on the research side of microbiology.

"If anyone has any additional questions, please come see me. Otherwise, this concludes my talk." I gave a quick nod and gathered up my papers as the crowd clapped.

I stepped off the stage and came down onto the main floor, shaking hands with various people. Off to the side, I eyed my travelling mates, two others from the university. Tonight, we'd planned on visiting the Space Needle, and checking out a few other hip places, and we were eager to let loose and have some fun. They gave me a quick wave, knowing I'd catch up with them at supper.

As I was chatting with a Director of Microbiology and another research technician, I spotted him. I wasn't sure where he came from, but in the blink of an eye, Theo was making his way down the aisle in my direction. Not wanting a confrontation here, I over-shook the hand I was holding. "Thank you for coming, Dr. Weisenhower."

"Great speech, Miss Richardson." Theo addressed me before I, or the two I was speaking with, had a chance to run.

"Thanks." I forced myself to look anywhere else but his eyes. Instead, I focused on the suit he wore, form-fitting in a nice shade of grey. The white shirt underneath wasn't anything spectacular, but his tie was. It had the caduceus symbol as well as tiny stethoscopes all over it. Being so close to him, even if I was still upset from our last run-in, had the power to increase my internal temperature, and suddenly the room was too hot. I wanted to shake out of my own suit jacket and fan myself.

Theo spoke as though I was the only one in the room. "I think your thoughts on genetic testing are spot on, however, would you really want to know if you are carrying the gene that causes a specific type of cancer?" The tone was even and calm, and it warmed the depths of my soul to hear it again. However, it was marred with a critical questioning of what he was doing here, at my speech.

I tipped my head to the side and tucked some of my hair behind my ear, casually glancing at the two people standing beside me. I stepped back just enough to put a respectable distance between Theo and myself. "Are you asking me personally?" Without making eye contact, my gaze roved over his unshaven face, seeing the twitch in the corner of his mouth.

"Generally speaking." Theo didn't even look at the other two ladies.

I exhaled a puff of air. "I think it would help a lot of people prepare. If they know they have a predisposition to breast cancer, for example, they can be proactive in their approach and do their part to prevent it happening."

The Director of Microbiology piped up. "Why wouldn't you want to find out? Especially if you have that lineage?"

Theo answered her but kept his focus on me. "Wouldn't that change their quality of life? What if they are at a predisposition and it so happens that they never end up getting it, then they've maybe missed out on something really fun and interesting, all because they had a marker for it, but it never activated."

My heart beat rapidly, and I was getting tingles in my arms. It didn't matter that I was still upset with him, my body was telling a vastly different story than my mind was, and I hated its natural reaction to him. I inhaled sharply, trying my best to dispense my energy. "I guess that's a choice they'll have to make, but I suppose if they are coming in for genetic testing, then they've already made that decision."

"Wouldn't you want to know?" The lab tech, a lady I'd peg at a few years older than me, spoke to Theo. She moved herself closer to him and was eyeing him like the eye candy he was.

"Personally, no. I don't think I'd want to know." He rocked back and forth on his heels.

I narrowed my eyes ever so. "Really?"

"Some things are worth going into blindly." There was a knowing smile and a telling wink. If he was trying to charm the pants off me, I wasn't having it.

So, I channeled the double entendre back into the scientific conversation, having had this discussion with fellow researchers previously. We were all in agreement that it would be better to know and prepare than to find out later we had cancer and had no idea we were genetically predisposed. Finding out earlier could give you the opportunity to build your resources and make the preparations ahead of time. "Respectfully, I disagree, especially about this."

"And that's what I like about you." There was a twinkle in his eye. "I'm Theo by the way." He extended his hand, shaking those of the two others before wrapping his fingers around my hand.

I tried to hold myself together, unsure if I should be amused or what. Was he mocking the other guests I'd just chatted with? In keeping up with the charade, I hesitantly shook his hand which he held a little longer than the others. It was soft and warm and instantly sent tantalizing tingles through my extremities. Damn my body. "Pleasure to meet you, Theo." My mouth was as dry as a desert, but the tumbleweeds rolled along in my head.

A wide grin crossed his face.

My gaze flipped quickly to the two colleagues who'd stepped back just enough to look ready to walk away, but close enough to hang around if the conversation suited them.

In keeping with the presumption of us being strangers, I stared at my ex-husband with a quizzical look on my face. This act – his confident demeanor, that award-winning smug little grin – it was all part of the charming

Theo I'd come to know and fall in love with. "You look rather familiar," I told the good doctor, and focused my energies on maintaining my distance, both physical and emotional. My head tilted from side-to-side, and a deep-rooted tenseness formed in my gut.

He tipped his nose into the air and looked around. Charming wouldn't even be the right word for it, but it sure was cute and a smidge confident in its execution. Enough to soften my heart just a tad. "Maybe because I'm an ass. And everyone remembers those guys."

"How's that?" Relief washed over me at his admission and the guilty expression that wiped the confidence off his face.

"I'll need to jump back in time a bit. You see, there was this amazing lady I was married to, but it sadly fell apart. Turns out one shouldn't get married when one is uber-drunk."

"That's good advice." There was more I wanted to add, but Theo didn't appear like he was ready to stop, so I let him splutter out his monologue. I needed answers.

"And this whip smart scientist, she took an interest in me, despite her better judgement, and somehow we became friends." A sparkle lit in his eyes, but slowly faded away, along with the promise of hope in his voice. "But work came between us, sadly, and we had to go our separate ways."

"Sometimes things like that happen."

"Maybe, but I think she was trying to get in touch with me. Maybe wanted to see us get back together or something like that, at least until one unfortunate night when I ended up being a huge ass to her. The last time I saw her," he leaned closer, "I did the unthinkable. In my deep-seated anger over her choosing her career over me, I accused her of doing things that were not true, and I know my actions hurt her as much as my words. I scarred her deeply."

The lump of discomfort and pain that had formed that night rebuilt its intensity, and I found it near impossible to swallow. A ribbon of disgust wove through me, and I tore my gaze away from those deep brown eyes of his, that were commanding my undivided attention.

But we were still talking about the situation in the third person, so I let that steer our conversation. Obviously, he was trying to have a personal conversation without getting too personal, even if it should *be* personal. "Have you tried telling her this?"

He shrugged. "She won't take my calls, my emails. Refused to accept two flower deliveries as well."

Well, the third worked – when he sent it to the office at Merryweather-Weston and the receptionist accepted on my behalf. They were gorgeous and smelled so nice.

But that wasn't going to fix anything. He could send all the flowers in the world. I needed to hear the truth. I needed to hear the words. So, I threw caution to wind. To hell with subtlety and dodging the elephant in the room. I surveyed the area; we were all alone, aside from a couple of hotel workers straightening out the chairs. I inhaled a breath of courage and exhaled a morsel of doubt. My arms folded across my chest, trying to stop the incessant cardiac pounding. "Do you blame me for not answering?" There, I was going to make it personal.

It was subtle, but he shook his head, taking a step closer to me. "Not at all. But I had to see you again, Izabella, and in person, in such a way that you'd hear me out." His voice carried an air of remorse as he stared down at the floor. "I was so stupid, and my actions were completely uncalled for. For the rest of my life, I'll regret being so…"

"Pigheaded? Mean? Hurtful?" The words flew out before I could stop them, but my hand flew to my lips and covered them up before others could escape.

"All of those things." Sadness crossed his face, and he tucked his hands into the pockets of his suit pants.

"Your words cut like a knife that night."

"I'm sorry. I'm so sorry."

There were the words I'd wanted to hear, and yet, I wasn't satisfied, or convinced. Not yet.

However, he seemed to shrink before my eyes as he rolled his shoulders inward and his head lowered. "I have no real explanation why I acted like a complete asshole, aside from the fact that I get these overwhelming tendencies of jealousy when my family is involved. I know what they think of you…"

My eyes widened at the thought.

"Trust me, it's all good. But seeing you there that night, so welcome and accepted, it bugged me. Instantly. All my life I've tried to fit in, despite my different career aspirations and everything else that makes me the black sheep of the Breslin Clan. Yet you waltzed in there, and bam, they can't wait to bend over backwards and help you." It wasn't hard to miss the undercurrent of jealousy in his tone.

"So, what you're saying is your anger was grossly misplaced? That it wasn't me you were mad at, it was your family's reaction to me?"

His cheeks flushed with crimson as I stared at them. "Yes, it was because I was so jealous, Izabella, and for that, I'm so very sorry." He pulled his hands free of his jacket and allowed them to hang limply at his sides.

Those words again, but this time, I felt the pain of him saying them. It wasn't just lip service, he meant them.

"That night, and many evenings afterward, I'd lay in bed and wonder if you'd ever want to see me again? I wondered if you thought I was some sort of Jekyll and Hyde figure, which I can assure you, I'm not normally." He fought the weak grin forming, swallowing it away. "Then, one night, I was consumed by a horrible thought." His Adam's apple bobbed, and a bad feeling flickered inside me, causing me to search out his face. "I wondered…" He inhaled sharp enough to steal my own breath away. "If you wished you'd never met me at all?"

While my body remained as still as a statue, my jaw unhinged and dropped. I blinked slowly and swallowed, trying to bring some much-needed moisture to my dry-as-a-bone mouth. "Oh, Theo." I inhaled and lifted his chin with the pad of my finger. An overwhelming urge commanded me to peer into the depths of his eyes, if for no other reason than he could see into mine and know where my heart lay. I focused harder into his soul than I'd ever had into a microscope. "Honestly," I breathed out deeply as a small smile formed. "You were the best mistake I'd ever made." A weird sensation fluttered in my heart; it lightened as if a weight had been removed. "Yeah, that night, you hurt me, and I'd tried to justify your reasonings, and failed. The betrayal was so inten-"

"You felt betrayed?" He slumped even further.

I gave him a half-hearted grimace. "Yeah. Even though we'd spent so little time together, in the grand scheme of things, I found myself feeling so many more emotions than I thought I ever could with someone I'd essentially just met. And you, you were this amazing guy, someone who was so open and honest about your feelings, it scared me to hear it. Even if it was all true and mirrored my own feelings. So, I rationalized with myself that you were too good to be true, and I had to let you go. And that night, that horrible night, I'm not ashamed to say that I enjoyed being with your family but when you told me I needed to find my own family, I was crushed, as I hadn't seen it like that. I believed I was there as a client, until you said those words. And even though you were mad, they were true. And that scared me."

His facial expression softened, and a flicker of hope dashed across as a smile started forming. "So why did you avoid my calls then?"

"Stupid self-loathing. I figured you wouldn't want to be with someone who did dream about all those things. I guess, deep down, I'm a girl with huge desires." I twisted the toe of my shoe into the carpet. "I want the family gatherings, I need to know I have a safe place to fall. I want siblings, as all my life I'd grown up envious of those with a brother or a sister, someone who understands what you're going through." A dull ache spread across my chest and my vision blurred. "I want a mother again, and I want a father since I never had one." As much as I loved and adored my family, I was selfish to want more, to be more mainstream. I swallowed hard and chanced a glance up into his face. "But most of all, I wanted you."

He beamed, and then the smile fell to the floor. "Wanted?"

"After that night, I felt like maybe I'd misread the whole thing, you courting me and maybe I was convinced that true love was as a foreign a concept to me as was hanging out with a family." I shook my head. "Throughout this whole crappy situation of needing the annulment, the one constant was you. I wanted you, I just wished the work part hadn't been such a major wedge in all of it. And had Grandpa never died, I would've never been thrust into that mess, I would've stayed with you and made a life with us. Everything about us feels natural and right."

"I wholeheartedly agree." He straightened himself up to his full height. "Can you ever forgive me for being such an ass that night? I swear, it's not a behaviour I'll ever repeat."

I took in his words and let them grow in my heart.

"Will you forgive me for not having had admitted my feelings? For putting the family business above love?"

"I asked you first." That sweet smile reappeared and melted my heart.

"I forgive you." That was the truth, and with those words came a relief in my heart I'd neglected to let go. I needed Theo, with all his desires and faults. He was the one I was meant to be with, even if our meeting got off to an unconventional start.

He stepped closer, nary a breath of wind could pass between us. "And I forgive you for loving me and my family so much."

Head tipped down, he lowered his lips to hover over mine. The heat rolled off him and my body warmed with a fresh wave of tingles. I reached up and placed my hand tenderly on the back of his neck and pulled him close. The desire to make up for lost time was more than I could stand.

A solid throat clearing from the conference room attendant brought me back down to Earth. "Sorry, I need to finish cleaning up in here."

"Of course." I couldn't take my eyes off my incredible ex-husband.

Theo beamed with a fresh new blush. "I'd love to discuss this new development further with you, Miss

Izabella Richardson. Can I interest you in a drink? The hotel bar makes a lovely cosmopolitan." He lifted his hand, his palm up.

"To hell with the drink. Want to go to the top of the Space Needle and have some adrenaline-based fun?"

"I'm not sure my adrenal glands could handle that right now, but I'm always up for a little cardio workout. Would you care for something a little more personal and soul-touching?"

"Since it's with you, I'm all in." I gave his hand a squeeze. "I love you."

"Just remember who said it first." He winked as we walked out the exit, ready to take on the world.

Epilogue

Two years later

I fell backwards on the bed in a suite of the Bellagio Hotel. Four intense days of conferences, but this time I wasn't here as a headliner or as a guest speaker. For the first time in three years, I was here to take in as many speakers as I could and then lose myself in the sights and sounds of the Vegas nightlife.

The company had long been sold, and my future with my own research lab was strong. I hadn't yet made the discovery I was hoping for, but I was close. So close. However, we had taken many new strides into molecular biology, and presented our findings to our colleagues. Things were looking up, and I couldn't be happier.

Well, almost, couldn't be.

Theo fell on the bed bedside me. "You should've been at that last speaker. He was insane and inspiring."

"Who was that?"

"Dr. Gunter Weirberger."

The name rang a bell, but that was it.

"Are you tired?"

I rolled over and looked at him. "What did you have in mind?"

"Figured we could walk the strip." That had become part of our yearly conferences, well, at least the last two. The first one we had together, we didn't remember much about.

"Can I change into something a little more fun?" Yes, I was already wearing comfy clothes designed for spending lots of time sitting down, but if we were going to be walking the strip and enjoying ourselves, I wanted to fit the part. Tonight was going to be fun, as I had something planned for later.

"Can I watch?" He wiggled his brows and walked over to wrap his arms around my waist.

"Then we'll never leave."

"That works too."

"And break tradition?"

He kissed me on the tip of my nose and let go. "Fine, get changed. We can eat up on Freemont Street."

I kicked off my plain Jane shoes and opened the closet door. "Something fun, eh?" Freemont was a blast last year, and I couldn't wait to party again under the overhead light show. What to wear? There was a cute pair of shorts and a off the shoulder top. But that wasn't perfect. I did bring two dresses for fancier outings. One of them would work. It was a silky full-length dress. It was long enough to be pretty and breezy enough to be alluring, and the cream colour was perfect against my tanned skin.

A few minutes later, both of us dressed for the evening, we headed out to the strip and took in the fountains in front of our hotel. As impressive as they were from the view in our room, they were simply magnificent up close and personal.

"Have you ever been up in the Eiffel Tower?" Theo leaned against the railing, his back to the dancing water show.

I turned and stared up the golden-coloured attraction. It was the least thrill-ride attraction on the strip. "Never." Usually we stuck to the heart-stopping rides at the Stratosphere or New York. "And we still need to cross Insanity off our list." We figured going at night would add extra wow to the ride. To see the strip lit up would be quite the sight.

"Paris isn't wild, but the view must be impressive."

I tipped my head back toward the hotel. "We have an impressive view of the strip. Remember?" Last night we turned the couch toward the brightly lit road and dimmed the lights in the room, making love repeatedly with the strip in full view. It was enchanting.

"Touché." He turned back to the fountains, the lights casting a glow on his handsome face. "So, no Eiffel Tower?"

I shook my head, I had other ideas in mind.

After crossing off a few rides on our vacation bucket list, we walked north and turned off the Strip. It wasn't as busy here and the crowds were certainly less.

"This place looks familiar." I stopped in front of the rundown chapel where two years ago, Theo and I exchanged vows.

Theo whistled. "Wow, I'm surprised it's still standing."

The stucco was chipped and the paint around the door and windows was peeling and faded. In a city where everything seemed to be constantly torn down and re-built, it was surprising it had been untouched. Like a scar, it remained.

We walked closer to the chapel while I shook my head. "We had so many things missing from our ceremony."

"Like what?" Theo squeezed my hand tight.

"Well…" I turned to gaze into his face. "We never had witnesses, at least none that we knew." It was law to have someone, but I thought it was the receptionist and some other random stranger who attended the ceremony. Their sketchy signatures and names were unrecognizable.

"That's true." He nodded.

"And you never had any family in attendance." However, I doubted the chapel would've held his entire family, but still. Maybe a few guests. "And a wedding song? What would we consider our song to be?"

He rubbed his chin. "Do we really need a song?"

So far in our time together, we still hadn't found that perfect song to sum up our relationship like so many of our friends had. "Fine, a song I could let slide. But what about rings? Never had those."

"Like this?" He pulled from his pocket a beautiful solitaire rose-gold ring.

My mouth fell open as the diamond sparkled under the streetlight, casting rays all around me. The sight of the ring caused me to laugh. "Actually, I meant like this." From deep within the zipped pocket of my dress, I presented Theo with a ring for him I'd spent hours searching for. A solid gold band with diamonds inset around it.

This time, Theo gasped. "Great minds think alike."

"Yes, they do." I took a quick glance back to the rundown chapel and tipped my head towards it. "What do you say? Want to get married?"

"Right now? What about all the other things we were missing from the first wedding?" His face said yes, but his tone said no.

"Oh right. That." I tried to contain my smile with a fake frown, while I stared at the entrance of the chapel. I waved.

Spilling out from the doors were Mr. and Mrs. Breslin, Natalie and Theo's oldest brother, Robert, and his wife, as well as my two best friends and their spouses.

"What?" Theo beamed.

I giggled.

"You planned this?"

Pride radiated out of me. It had been tough planning it all, but it had worked out. "Guilty. We'd been talking about getting married again for a while, but hadn't narrowed anything down. Mission accomplished. Are you okay with this?"

He looked toward the group of people heading over to us. "I couldn't imagine anything more perfect." He bent his head down and planted the most romantic kiss on my expectant lips, and I savoured the sweet taste of him.

"I love you so much, Izabella."

"And I love you, Theo."

My plan had worked out perfectly. I was in the

place where I'd originally met the love of my life, at the place where we'd first exchanged vows. This time, I wasn't just marrying the hot guy I enjoyed hanging out with at the convention, I was marrying my best friend. And this time, my name would be spelled correctly, and with the addition of Breslin attached to it.

Life couldn't get any better.

Or could it?

Dear Reader

WOW – did you love that ending?

Coming up next is a fun novella titled *Whistler's Night.* A sweet, second chance romance. If you'd like a sneak peek on my upcoming projects please join my mailing list. I promise not to spam you (they come every two weeks) and to keep things brief with lots of freebies, (including a scavenger hunt). Your time is valuable, and I appreciate how you've spent time reading my story. Thank you for that!

As an author, it makes my day when a reader or blogger share their thoughts on the characters they've spent time with. When readers fall in love with a character, it's encouraging to write more. Fun fact, when I finished writing *Duly Noted* and released it, a lot of readers wanted to know more about the friendship between Lucas and Aurora, and because of those emails, *That Summer* came to be.

So, if you don't mind, share with me what you liked, what you loved, or even what you didn't like. I'd love to hear from you via email, my website, or a review on your favourite retailer site. It doesn't have to be long, even just as simple as "Glad Theo and Izabella worked things out, or Theo is my new book boyfriend" works. Reviews and ratings help me gain visibility, and as I'm sure you can tell from my books, reviews are tough to come by. If you have the time for an extra review, I'd love a review/rating on Goodreads and/or BookBub.

Thank you so much for spending time with me.

Yours,

H.M. Shander

Other Books

By USA TODAY bestselling author H.M. Shander

The Courting of Charlotte Cooper set

Run Away Charlotte

Ask Me Again

The Aurora MacIntyre Trilogy

Duly Noted

That Summer

If You Say Yes

The Ladies of Westside Series

Serving Up Innocence

Serving Up Devotion

Serving Up Secrecy

Serving Up Hope

Accidentally In Love series

It All Began with a Note

It All Began with a Mai-Tai

It All Began with a Wedding

Acknowledgements

This is my twelfth thank you in the back of a book, and I swear, writing these never gets easier. Terribly afraid to miss someone, or a category will be left out. And then I wonder, does anyone even read these? I know as an author, I do, but I wonder if readers do? Writing a book feels like a solo endeavour, until you start listing all the support and cheerleading along the way. I couldn't be here without the help of these truly fantastic people.

First – my Shander family, whom you may know on my social media platforms as Hubs, The Teen, and Little Dude. You guys rock and encourage me to make my dreams a reality. Thank you for letting me hit my daily word counts, or to inquire about preorders or who my characters are, I appreciate you being as invested in this as I am. Thank you for your constant help, your unending support and all your love. I love you all with my whole heart.

To my parents and in-laws and extended family – Thank you for your support, endless cheerleading, and encouraging your friends and family to give my books a try. Having you visit me at markets and book signings means the world. I have an amazing family, and every day I'm thankful to you all. Thanks for being you.

To Mandy - as soon as those first chapters are written, you are my go-to gal. You let me know what works, what isn't, and if those opening lines, pages and chapters are enough to hook a reader into wanting more and I'm so appreciative of that. It's great having you to bounce an idea or two (or a couple hundred) and you are such a fantastic mentor and cheer squad. I heart you more than you'll ever know.

To Josephine - thanks for spending your free time

reading my words and pointing out what didn't make sense and what needed to be expanded on, and how you enjoyed Izabella and could tell when she was acting out of character. Your critiques are as welcome as your unending enthusiasm. I look forward to being your cheerleader when the time comes.

To Megan. That cover is the perfect image of Theo and Izabella, and I can't imagine seeing them any other way. Great job! I'm so thrilled we worked on this together, and I look forward to many more covers designed by you.

To Irina. Thanks for your dedication to fixing my errors and highlighting the inconsistencies. It never ends, but I think I'm getting better. At least I'm not making the same mistakes time and time again. LOL.

To Victoria. Thank you for your dedication to proofread Wedding, to catch the corrections I missed and for doing it within the time frame needed. You are a superstar, and I hope we'll work together again.

If I missed you, it certainly wasn't intentional. I know I couldn't be where I am without the help of so many others. Thank you! And thank you for reading and making it all the way to the end. You all rock.

About the Author

H.M. Shander is a star-gazing, romantic at heart who once attended Space Camp and wanted to pilot the space shuttle, not just any STS – specifically Columbia. However, the only shuttle she operates in her real world is the #momtaxi; a reliable SUV that transports her two kids to school and various sporting events. When she's not commandeering Betsy, you can find the elementary school librarian surrounded by classes of children as she reads the best storybooks in multiple voices. After she's tucked her endearing kids into bed and kissed her trophy husband goodnight, she moonlights as a contemporary romance novelist; the writer of sassy heroines and sweet, swoon-worthy heroes who find love in the darkest of places.

If you want to know when her next heart-filled journey is coming out, you can follow her on Twitter(@HM_Shander), Facebook (hmshander), or check out her website at www.hmshander.com.Thanks for reading– all the way to the very end.

Manufactured by Amazon.ca
Bolton, ON

14646754R10155